THE CONQUEROR

Rich Parsons & Tony Keaveny

Michael O'Mara Books Limited

DEDICATION

We would like to dedicate this book to our daughters who were born in 1993.

To Eve and Annabelle

Also to John, Luke, Elizabeth, Kelly and Alice for all the child benefit. And to Dianne and Helen without whom the above would not have been possible.

First published in Great Britain in 1995 by
Michael O'Mara Books Limited
9 Lion Yard, Tremadoc Road
London SW4 7NQ

A CIP catalogue record for this book is available from the British Library

ISBN 1-85479-962-2

Typeset by DP Photosetting, Aylesbury, Bucks
Printed and bound in England by Cox & Wyman, Reading

CONTENTS

If you would like to join the Friends of the Conqueror Society (FOCS) write to Rich Parsons and Tony Keaveny care of Michael O'Mara Books, 9 Lion Yard, Tremadoc Road, London SW4 7NQ.

ILLUSTRATIONS

All in full colour unless otherwise stated below.

THE PROLOGUE

And in the beginning was the Word.
And the Word was 'Congratulations'.
And the Word became a phrase.
And the phrase was 'Congratulations, Mister and Missus Almighty. You have lovely, healthy twin boys. But then I guess you already knew that, being Omnipotent and Omniscient and Omnipresent'.

Thus did it come to pass that these spawn of the Almighties became known as God Almighty and Sylvester Almighty.

And when they did come of atom-smashing and molecule-creating age did they give up the spare room with bunk beds and washbasin and were they each given a universe by their parents. And these universes were parallel.

And lo, during one particularly violent family argument were they told in no uncertain terms to go forth and multiply and did they so do.

And did God Almighty, being the elder of the twins by two minutes, get first choice of planetary name using the five letters of creation. Hence did it come to pass that his creation was called Earth.

And did Sylvester content himself with the name Threa for his first creation.

But verily, as did God create oceans, and flora and fauna and mountains and fjords and valleys and golf courses on his green and pleasant lands, did Sylvester sub-contract by creating his own planetary Gods of Vegetation – twins as it happens – and Gods of Animal Life, to do the work for him while he took his celestial washing home at weekends.

And it came to pass that Earth learnt of Threa by the supernatural receipt of *The Chronicles Of Ancient Threa*, volumes one, two and three.

Yea verily forsooth did the fourth such volume chronicle the ascendancy of the evil Tharg Empire. Twin-headed, four-armed travellers of the Cosmos, Thargs claimed Threa and the surrounding Galaxy as their own.

But they were thwarted by the inter-Universal combo of the brawn of Krap the Conqueror, a Threan-born Barbarian of mighty, bulging musculature, and the brain of Colin, a simple Librarian from the planet Earth (Clacton Central Library and Reference Centre), whose knowledge of the *Chronicles of Ancient Threa* was second to none.

And alas, though Colin did return from his Cosmos-saving adventure, did Krap perish at the hands of Thong, an evil Tharg Emperor. And also did Susan die, she known as the Social Worker who was, is and forever more shall be, Colin's desire for lustful coupling.

Yet did Colin eat her, for was she dead and he in need of sustenance during his exile on Threa before discovering a portal to return to Earth.

And so was Threa and its parallel Universe once more plunged head-first into peace.

THE APRES-LOGUE

YE COMINGE OF YE BOOKE

Verily were the Gods of animal creation – of all that crawls and runs and flies and generally craps on other things (hereinafter known as the Bestial Gods) – in mortal combat with the twin Gods who shall be collectively known as Yoof. The Yoof twins were responsible for everything green and wavy and woody with leaves. The Bestials, Gods of all animals (including the not so nice ones such as snails and slugs and worms and xenophobic toads) wished to control the planet, crush the Yoof twins and extend their influence over the Galaxy, and Sylvester was under the influence at the time thus knowing nothing of what occurred.

But alas and alack, did disaster strike in the formerly balanced war of Nature and natural things.

And was that disaster in the shape of a book that came into the possession of the Bestial Gods. And the book was full of incomprehensible runes and hieroglyphics and pictures of bipeds doing unspeakable things to one another.

And lo, did some Gods, especially Hump the Camel God and Roger the Cat God, declare this book-shaped thing to be the product of the generations past of the planet Threa and that it did encapsulate the learnings from all Ages past to present.

And yet did others say that this book must be a present from the all-highest, or at any rate that God who shall remain nameless but who in any case did create the very first spark of life in the Universe (except for himself who was already sparking).

And the name of this book was, in the Threan language, *The Blue Peter Annual 1978*. And lo, did the Bestial Gods follow most carefully the words written therein inscribed: 'How to make a Blue Peter Advent Crown'. And thus did they create a monstrous machine so powerful that from the smallest of atoms could it reproduce an entire being with much smoking and rumbling and belching were it to be a smoking, rumbling and belching creature, and with much squeaking were it to be a squeaker.

And struthe, did ye Gods rub their hands with unrestrained glee and cackle at ye Gods of Vegetation, who by now did realize that something be very seriously amiss and it did look like they be in big trouble.

For did the Gods of Everything Bestial decide to up the tempo on ye olde vegetation killing game and thereby grab the Balance of Nature by the throat, thus becoming so powerful that one day they might even challenge on a Universal basis he who shall remain nameless but who shall, in the interim, be known as Sylvester Almighty, Creator of All.

And were the Gods of Vegetation not even given access to this terrible machine at weekends. And thus was the Balance of Nature undone and did Chaos rear its ugly head on Threa.

CHAPTER ONE

1). One plus one is plum.
2). The square of the hypotenuse is equal to the sum of the square
of the amount of money in my jockstrap.
(Trainee chaos mathematician Sylvester answering question eight
of his final examination paper way back in the mists of time.)

'Art thou coming down for t'breakfast, Young 'un?' His father's voice shocked Colin away from the mirror. His morning ritual of deciding whether the black spots on his face were hairs trying to push through or just blackheads as he suspected came to an abrupt halt.

Damn! he thought. Twenty-two today and still no need to shave. The whispy down-like hairs protruding from his chin still numbered only in their tens, and showed no signs of multiplying, nor indeed of lengthening beyond the centimetre or so they had struggled through so far.

'You don't have t'shout in my ear, father, you could quite easily call from downstairs,' complained Colin, continuing the daily conversation.

'What, and wake up t'neighbours?' boomed his father.

As his father disappeared downstairs, Colin looked at the mirror again and slumped forward in despair. He remembered doing this last year on his twenty-first birthday, and every day since. Nothing changed. He was still the same dandruff-ridden, spot-erupting five-foot-two mess that he had been then.

He smoothed down his unkempt hair and turned side-on to the mirror, swivelling his eyes to look at his profile. There was something Greek ... no, Roman, and statuesque about him in this pose, but coming round to look at himself face-on it was lost. He shrugged his shoulders and turned away.

He pulled on yesterday's shirt after sniffing the armpits and deciding that if he didn't run anywhere today it could last him another couple of days. Not that he did ever run anywhere.

Colin thought about that day exactly a year ago, the start of his adventures on Threa, a planet light-years away from Earth yet just around the corner in a parallel Universe. Or something like that. Anyway, three volumes of history had been published about the place and Colin had helped to write the fourth based on his own bitter experiences.

Colin had been *someone* there. With the help of an increasingly selective memory he recalled the camaraderie he had enjoyed with Krap the mighty Conqueror, until Krap was killed by the Thargs; the glint of a relationship with Susan the Social Worker, until he had had to eat her. Colin alone had ended the threat of Tharg ascendancy on Threa and possibly over the whole universe.

And yet try telling that to anyone on Earth and they just laughed at you, even though the fourth volume of *The Chronicles Of Ancient Threa* had just been miraculously published and 'The Librarian' was a central character – though it didn't actually use Colin's name. Colin's flipping co-author Wealthy Vicars must have erased it throughout after Colin had returned to Earth. Nobody believed that he, Colin, was a super-hero on another world. Nobody actually believed he was anything but the Assistant Helper to the Librarian's Assistant at Clacton Central Library and Reference Centre, and they all treated him as such.

At night he would dream he was standing in front of a thousand-strong audience at the Albert Hall, describing his adventures on Threa, telling them how brave he was and how he had been a most important person in the scheme of things in this galaxy and others. In his dream everything would go well until someone would put his hand up as if to ask a question. Colin would point to him and he would stand up and address the crowd loudly – louder than Colin ever could. Colin would then realize that nobody was interested in him any more, and wake up sadder and lonelier than when he had gone to bed after another sad and lonely day.

And even Susan had left. His stomach cramped as he remembered the Susan who had re-appeared after Colin had eaten her on Threa. She was so ... so ... so sexy and vital and she had that shimmering ... shimmering what? Well, just a shimmering thing. She had become an exotic dancer at the Piper Club and then moved out of the area without letting Colin know where she was headed; in fact, without ever saying another word to him at all.

Colin was growing up, and with that came the realization that his life was not really dynamic, or vibrant. Were there some things about it he would like to change? Maybe it had been a mistake coming back from Threa so quickly? But as he shrugged on his battered tweed jacket he pushed all these thoughts from his mind, as he always did before setting off to work.

At the foot of the stairs a cup whistled past his head and smashed against the wall.

'Sorry lad, it slipped,' said his father, standing at the sink six yards away.

Colin wondered why his father employed a Yorkshire accent, having lived all his life in Clacton, and why his mother was never home for breakfast. He shut the door behind him and walked down the steps to the street.

The walk to the Clacton Central Library and Reference Centre hadn't changed, which was no great surprise as Colin and his parents hadn't moved home and the Library hadn't been relocated elsewhere in the sprawling urban mass which was Clacton. He arrived at 9.15 a.m. on the dot as usual. He mumbled 'Hello' to Brian, who was silently bouncing around the library tidying a book here, and a shelf there, and went through to the office to hang up his jacket.

He waited a moment for the next part of the routine; Brian arrived on cue, stuck his stupid grinning face through the door and said,' Try not to lose any more books, eh Colin? Har snort.'

Colin smiled weakly. He had mislaid a copy of *The Blue Peter Annual 1978*, which he used to cover his furtive reading of the *National Geographic* during his break periods. In a hurry one day to resume his shift on the check-out he had placed it on top of the Crime and Catastrophe section bookcase for later, but when he returned it had gone. Just vanished.

Brian had discovered the gap during his weekly stock-check and claimed in a manic whisper that it was the first book he had ever lost from any one of his libraries. Although Colin had paid for the missing volume from his wages, he was reminded every morning about this momentary lapse of concentration, and it just became part of his life.

Today, though, Colin didn't have time to spend a few minutes in the toilet while the tears flowed. Brian came back to the office in a mad hurry and came as close as he ever would to shouting.

'Every man to the pumps, young Colin,' he hissed. 'Chop, chop, to the check-out desk. Queues are forming and I'm afraid I have to complete my monthly audit report. Need you there, snort snort.'

Stuff your head up a sheep's bottom, thought Colin vehemently.

'Be right there Brian,' said Colin meekly as he walked towards the check-out desk. He sat in his chair, deliberately opened his ink-pad, pushed the date stamp into the pad and tested it on the blotter in front of him. He loved the feeling of power as he knew that a fair-sized queue of people was watching him, impatient to have their books stamped and be gone. But he also knew they were far too polite to say anything.

The stamp was correct, so he looked up brightly as he held out his right hand for the first book to be borrowed.

Mr Sick Bentburthy handed over *Trials and Tribulations,* the only book he ever borrowed. Colin opened it at the first page and stamped it heavily. He snapped the book shut and handed it back to Mr Bentburthy with a sickly smile.

Colin had a little difficulty finding the inside front cover of Gemma Spasmo's *Black Beauty in the South African Townships,* but managed to recover by looking as if he were interested in the contents. He gave young Gemma a knowing nod and a superior quiver of his nostrils.

The Throbulet's *Chronicles of Ancient Threa,* volume

one, slipped through without a problem, as did the Throbulet's *Chronicles of Ancient Threa*, volume two, and the Throbulet's *Chronicles of* ... Hey! Wait a moment, he thought.

Looking up from his desk, Colin saw a Throbulet with an enormous hump on its back, holding out a gaudily jacketed romance. Colin recognized it as *Anthea Orgasms in Public Places*, but it suddenly occurred to him that Throbulets were Threan creatures, surely. He had just served three of them and here was a fourth and what would Brian say if he let out all these books to animals from another planet? Blimey! There'd be hell to pay if they didn't bring them back. And there was no guarantee that they even understood the Earth system of borrowing books anyway. And that hump – it could be full of books, and then where would that leave Colin?

'What's that hump on your back?' he asked the Throbulet suspiciously. If the animal gave him any grounds for concern he was going to go straight off to Brian and let him deal with it.

'Wings, I suppose,' answered the Throbulet awkwardly, thrusting the book forward for stamping as if it were rushed for time, or in trouble, or something.

'How do I know there's wings in that hump? Or more to the point how do you know there's wings in that hump?' persisted Colin.

'Let's just call it a hunch,' shrugged the Throbulet.

'OK,' riposted Colin, 'How do *you* know there's wings in that hunch? I've never seen a Throbulet fly, and none of the other – ' he looked around – 'thousand or so Throbulets here have a hunch of that ...' he tailed off, his mouth wide open at the sight of hundreds of Throbulets in his library. ACTUALLY IN HIS LIBRARY!

There were small ones, large ones, medium-sized ones and ones in-between. Some smiled at him, some just stared; others looked tired and strained. Most held copies of *The Chronicles of Ancient Threa* and the rest, guiltily, held Mills and Boon romances. Colin even spotted the odd *National Geographic* in there. Colin panicked.

What was he to do? How would Brian react to finding this horde of whispering extraterrestrial creatures in his library wanting to borrow half of his stock? They weren't theatening him or anything, but it just wasn't right. No, something was definitely wrong.

Get your stupid arse over here, he thought to Brian, who was still sitting in the office. 'Brian?' His voice was timid and strangled. It escaped only with a squeak. 'Brian?'

The Throbulets started to advance on the desk, showing their sexual organs in a display of annoyance, and chanting 'Stamp, stamp,' in a menacing whisper as they indicated the open front covers of their books.

Colin by now was wondering what to do about his underpants. His mother had always told him not to get run over in dirty ones, but this? She'd said nothing about this. How could she? And Colin didn't know what to do. He tried to scream, but not even air escaped from his tightened throat.

The Throbulets were climbing the front of his desk now, clambering over to get to him and his date stamp, which he held in a protectively clasped fist up by his right shoulder. They were after his stamp, with

7

which they would validate their own books and take them out of the library, probably still chanting 'Stamp, stamp.' Colin thought, it may be a dream, but ignored that idea. A test? What for? A problem? Yes, definitely.

Oh damn, he was about to be engulfed by the advancing Throbulets. Then a shining silver light streaked before his eyes and the advance slowed.

The invasion stopped for a second, the thingy-shaped faces looking concerned as if they had been interrupted during a bout of Oriental sex (work it out for yourself). Then another swish and this time Throbulet heads, together with demented grins, seemed to lift from the bodies and fly towards Colin. As he ducked the bodiless heads, Colin had a fleeting moment of recognition, but couldn't grasp what it was he recognized. Throbulets still piled over the desk, their temporary hesitation over, and shoved books at him, hissing 'Stamp, stamp'.

Colin was by now pressed hard against the back of the check-out area. His flesh crawled and his mouth worked overtime, trying to call Brian but to no avail as the fright which loosened his bowels severely constricted the upper part of his body. He sound-lessly glopped and gulped as a being descended from the ceiling, all in yellow with yellow skin, yellow tights, yellow tutu, yellow slippers, yellow wand, yellow hair, and a yellow mouth which opened and said ... nothing. The yellow head separated from the yellow body following another silver swish and yel-low blood spurted from the yellow neck towards Colin as the yellow head spiralled off towards the Romance section.

Colin instinctively took off his glasses to wipe them

clean of the plasma. His mind whirled and wouldn't keep still as he glimpsed, through the fuzzy myopia...

KRAP!!!!

Colin hastily replaced his spectacles and looked again. It couldn't be.

Krap was dead.

Krap was no more.

The Throbulets were real, and the yellow person and all that, but it couldn't be.....

Krap the Conqueror (for 'twas he), so cruelly slain by the Thargs on Threa almost an Earth year ago, was in the middle of a killing frenzy as he hacked and stabbed at the prone bodies of the invading Throbulets. Blood was spattered all over his blue pin-striped suit and his metal-rimmed glasses (which were not unlike Colin's), and sweat stained his brow. Even the white dress-shirt couldn't hide the rippling and pumping of his mighty muscles. Colin's jaw dropped open in amazement and a huge gob of pink flesh flew into it off the keen, slicing edge of Krap's broadsword. It made him gag and choke and spit it out and be violently sick all over a severed head. He tripped over the torso of an animal he could not name but which was not a Throbulet. Wiping his mouth with the bottom of his tie, Colin looked up at Krap, who was chopping up the hind quarters of one particularly large and pink version of the animal Colin had stumbled over.

'Just take enough skin for a new loin cloth, though pink's not my favourite colour, I must admit. H'mm, seems waterproof though, and it will be nice to get out of these heathen clothes.'

The voice, thought Colin, the killing frenzy, the

bloodcurdling screams, the broadsword. All Krap! But how?

'Hah!' spat the mighty barbarian, his massive hands on his hips and his shaggy mane thrown back. 'Of course 'tis me, oh puny one!

'By the way, did I ever tell thee about the traditional method of making loin cloths taken from a lesson by my old mucker the Warrior of Worthing?' Colin shook his head dumbly so Krap carried on talking while he carefully trimmed pieces of Throbulet.

'Well, this particular swarthy hero was always surrounded by bevvies of beauties whom he regularly manacled by the wrists, ankles and nipplerings during sado-masochistic sex sessions. But they always regarded him as a regular kind of guy with regular interests and habits.

'Anyway this method of making a loin cloth involves cutting the skin of an animal in a lattice pattern, then coating it with the discharge of the South American flat-footed fish called Mickelly. This process results in a breathable rain-resistant material that is not only warm to the touch but also lifts your testicles and separates them.'

'But ... but you're dead,' spluttered Colin. He was torn between fright and delight, excitement and amazement. He didn't understand or follow a word of what Krap had been saying. He knew not why the Conqueror was interested in lifting his testes, nor separating them. He knew about wedding rings and engagement rings, but how did you get a ring to stay on your nipple?

The only thing he was certain of was that before him was his old pal, Krap. He eventually gave in to the realization that the invasion of the library had not been a hallucination and he might have been killed had Krap been in the state in which Colin had last seen him, ie. dead.

And what was more, if he had had to stamp all those books, he would have surely suffered from Repetitive Strain Injury, or Repetitive Stamping Injury at the very least, and then where would he be when Brian found the books gone to another planet and Colin unable to work?

He shook with fright and delayed shock. Somewhat confused, he touched his nipples looking for rings. When Krap finished his lecture on loin cloths, he walked around to Colin's side of the desk. Slipping on the yellow blood, Krap slid across the floor and his knee slammed into Colin's seated groin. Pain forced its way up through Colin's body into his throat. With a final thought about lifted testicles, he spasmed and sank into oblivion.

CHAPTER TWO

'Real Madrid 3
'Surreal Madrid ...... chip hacksaw vaseline'
A famous inter-galactic league result (amateur dwarf-tossing).

As he came to, Colin vaguely remembered what had happened and felt very peculiar. Without opening his eyes or uncrossing his legs he wondered whether he should hope that the events of the past few minutes actually had occurred, or whether it was best to hope that they hadn't. His mind was eventually made up for him by the pain in his groin and the taste of a warm, thick, salty liquid dribbling into his mouth.

He lifted his head from the check-out desk. Krap was reviving him with Throbulet blood. He looked at Krap. Krap looked back at Colin, amusement on his face, broadsword by his side. He no longer wore a suit, but had a rather slimy-looking pink loin cloth on from which the original occupier's blood still dripped. It appeared to be stapled together, and indeed, Colin could see the discarded stapler on the floor, amongst the rubbery flesh, which had started to ooze pus in brown globules.

Before Colin could voice his questions Krap guffawed.

'Yes, oh Librarian, I can see that I shall indeed have to explain things to you. Come, to the Reference

Section of your Library, where we may parlay more easily without this,' he indicated the carnage with disdain, 'mess in the way.'

Colin automatically got up and moved out from behind the desk towards the Reference Section. He was in a daze. He pulled out his hanky from his pocket and started furiously rubbing his glasses clean of blood, and so missed seeing the mighty Krap slipping in the glutinous mess on the floor. Krap got sheepishly to his feet and followed Colin.

Colin sat at one of the reading desks. His mind was still a kaleidoscope of questions and queries. Little tingles of ... of ... well, of pleasure really, ran down his spine and turned to what was at this stage really a quite pleasant sort of pain between his legs. His hero was back from the grave! But how?

Krap towered over him, pectorals twitching, biceps straining and triaxials rippling, and boomed his booming guffaw.

'Patience, patience,' he bellowed, reading Colin's mind. 'I shall reveal all. But to speed things up I shall transmit mental images, for you to follow the story so far. Ready?'

Colin nodded dumbly.

'Then Librarian, stare at that conveniently blank white wall over there and I shall transmit the story.' Colin did as he was told.

A huge cow-like creature stood in a field. Its rear legs were pulled apart by thick chains, which were pinned to solid metal posts hammered into the ground. Its head was similarly tethered and its tail was strapped to its back.

The creature looked worried.

The picture went blank.

'Ah, er, sorry,' apologized Krap awkwardly. 'Um. . .
no, forget that. Ah, here we go.'

This time Colin saw what he could only surmise
was the planet Threa. Green, lush, rolling hills disappeared towards the horizon.

But there was something wrong, Colin could sense
that. The image zoomed to a bush nearby and it was
obvious that the leaves had been nibbled and were in
the first stages of decay. The grass around the bush
had been cropped, and an air of despair and
despondency hung over the environs, like a layer of
gravy on mashed potato. It all looked very sad
indeed.

Sub-titles appeared. 'Yes, Librarian, the Balance of
Nature on Threa is threatened. Vegetation is being
remorselessly destroyed,' they read.

The picture switched to a group of very old people
sitting around a book, next to a contraption covered in
tinsel, sticky-back plastic with a woodgrain design,
and with what appeared to be squeezy bottles sticking out of it at strange angles. The whole thing was
topped by a screen, which seemed to be made out of
old coat hangers. White capital letters with a hint of
green leapt out at Colin.'

'LET ALL YE BOW DOWN BEFORE THE GODS OF
ANIMAL LIFE
AND PRAY
THE BLUE PETER ANNUAL 1978
AND ADORE ON HIGH
THEIR GREAT DEEDS
AND EAT BABIES AND BURN PEOPLE.'

Colin gasped, and for some inexplicable reason felt
a tidal wave of guilt wash over him.

The old people, some dressed like men in long, flowing gowns, and some dressed like women, in long, flowing gowns, exuded old age and ancientness. One held a cast-iron bucket and seemed to be talking to it. They were laughing and smiling silently (there was still no sound to Colin's picture) and rubbing their hands with glee.

'Who's that with the bucket?' asked Colin. The picture wavered for a minute while Krap broke his concentration and answered.

' 'Tis Mantis, who be God of most Vertebrates, and whose icon be a figure praying,' he explained. 'In the bucket holds he his brother, Asian, God of all Invertebrates and a spineless example himself to the extent that he be carried around in a bucket. His icon be a crushed figure or animal.'

Krap turned to Colin. 'Thou meanest thou hast never heard of the temples of the crushed Asian and the praying Mantis before?' he asked incredulously. Colin hadn't, and turned his attention sheepishly back to the story.

One of the old Gods caught a passing chicken and ripped a leg off it with a strength that belied his puny appearance. He threw the leg into the contraption before him, as the de-legged chicken hopped off, silently squawking and falling over.

The old man played with the screen, and to Colin's utter amazement a chicken appeared right next to the machine. It had eight legs and four wings, but otherwise was an exact copy of the one who had lost a leg, and who was currently hopping in tight circles on the floor trailing its wings and trying to bite the old man's feet.

The new arrival looked about for a moment, then

flapped its wings and careered off-screen, tripping over its extra legs (two of which were on its head).

The old folk fell about with glee. One of their number lifted his robe, turned his buttocks to the machine and, Colin assumed, farted. Playing with the screen he created foaming tankards of beer, gallons of what looked like baked beans, a score of pickled onions and what appeared to be a small pile of dried plums. ('Prunes,' prompted Krap impatiently, 'prunes.')

The general mirth and merriment was extended to supping the ale and some handy bottles of wine, and soon all the old folk were blind drunk and asleep where they had sat.

From the left, two people tiptoed into shot. One, thought Colin incredulously, was a double of Harrison Ford, and the other was remarkably similar to Mel Gibson. They crept to the machine and placed something on it. The picture zoomed in once again and Colin realized that it was a toenail clipping. Just like the ones his Dad left in his (Colin's) bed every Friday afternoon.

Seconds later, Krap appeared in the picture.

He was stood in all his naked glory, and Colin saw that he, too, had a teeny tiny ... the picture panned out and Colin watched the Yoof twins, Gods of all things green and wavy, now disguised as two famous actors, issue instructions, arms waving.

Colin read on the subtitles what it was they were saying, 'Go, Krap Oh Mighty Reconstituted One, and save our Vegetation. Be our Champion, for Thargs there are a-plenty born of this machine most foul and hideous, and other animal monstrosities. Previously could the Bestial Gods make elephants, and camels, and large mice and OK things, but with this machine can they bring back the largest of creatures of bygone ages and with this comes the greatest destruction of vegetation and disruption of the Balance of Nature ever seen.'

At that moment one of the old people woke up. He hurriedly threw a handful of soil at the machine then hit the keyboard several times before collapsing once more.

Giant earthworms, smelsingborgs with twelve heads and Throbulets with enormous balls sprang into existence and chased away the two movie stars and the unarmed, unclothed Krap (all except the Throbulets whose balls precluded any quick movement). As they exited the picture, Harrison and Mel seemed to Colin to age a few hundred years. Strange, he thought, but there you go.

Colin's mind was released and he slumped back, stunned and dazed.

'That,' he gasped, 'is incredible. A DNA Accelerated Multiplier Unit! Wow!'

'Nay,' yelled Krap in an annoyed tone of voice, 'did not the Gods tell ye that 'tis a BLUE PETER ADVENT CROWN'.

'No, no,' said Colin. 'They've created a DNA Accelerated Multiplier Unit and can recreate matter from the smallest atom! Oh, I can't explain but it is absolutely incredible.'

Krap tossed his head in frustration and gave up.

'Call it what you bloody-well like, it has to be destroyed. We have to get to it and be done with it before the recreated Thargs can re-establish their empire, or create sexual organs for themselves and breed.' He shuddered at the thought. 'Why, they could even recreate Andrew the Spineless's vertebrae, or anything. The animal monstrosities could decimate the planet's vegetation, and completely bugger the environment. Think of that. For do we not have responsibility to the green and pleasant lands of Threa to ensure that the Balance of Nature be balanced and not, um, unbalanced and hence all the vegetation dead and stuff?'

Colin's mouth gaped open. 'We?' he asked.

'We,' laughed Krap gaily, 'for whilst I can, with my trusty broadsword, handle anything they throw at me...'

Except Thong the Third, thought Colin recalling the Tharg Commander who had killed Krap last year.

'... Bastard,' spat Krap, and continued. 'I have needs use of your encyo ... encyplo ... encople ... vast knowledge of the *Ancient Chronicles* to discover the whereabouts of the machine. For have the Gods moved it for safe keeping, to that mythical homeland of the Thargs, the Isla St Clair.'

Immediately, and to Krap's obvious satisfaction as he read Colin's thoughts, Colin's mind spun to page 721, volume two, *Chronicles of Ancient Threa*.

'And yea verily did the Thargs have a homeland which shall hereafter and everafter be referred to as their homeland, and that place was called and shall forever after be called the Isla St Clair, for be-it surrounded by water and be off the local coast.'

'But I don't understand,' whined Colin, still mystified. 'How shall I guide you there? The Chronicles say nothing about the Isla's location. They talk about the map references for Sharon Island, or is it Tracey Island, and even the Isla Low U 2 wip Me, but not the Isla St Clair.'

'And when you say the Warrior of Worthing,' he continued, 'there's no Worthing mentioned in the Chronicles. Do you mean *Worthing* Worthing?' He had decided to get all his questions out now so that he understood the situation before jumping into it, or being pushed into it, which was the more likely scenario.

'Aye, Librarian, Worthing of your world,' replied the Conqueror with a gleam in his eye.

'But how?' asked Colin.

'As you saw, I was sent by the Gods, the Immortals, the Creators of all that is Vegetable and green and good and non-violent – except for the Aspidistran Flowering Person Eater, which was an early if hardy effort – to guard the portal which doth exist at thine library. The crossing point for our worlds and times and cosmoses. Or is it cosmii?'

'But why?' persisted Colin. He was still bemused. 'If you were recreated by this machine, why didn't you destroy it there and then?'

Krap looked sad for a moment. 'Forsooth, ye Yoof twins did hope that the machine could be used for purposes good and selfless and holy. For yea, had they been persecuted 'tis true, but they do believe that there be good in everyone and they did hope that somewhere, sometime, a little of that goodness would show in the minds of the creators of the BLUE PETER ADVENT CROWN.' He spat on the floor in distaste. 'So did they give the Bestial Gods a head start.' He spat again. He started to look decidedly distraught now and shook his head in despair before continuing.

'But alas did the power become too much, and as a compatriot of yours once said, "Absolute power is a corruption of boo slut reepaw." For did mine creators

20

realize that, should this power be mishandled, so would the portals be threatened, either to spread the foulness to other worlds or else to recapture all external knowledge of the planet Threa and the Isla St Clair so that they,' he spat once more,' could get on with their dastardly attack on the Balance of Nature on Threa and the subsequent re-establishment of the Tharg race.'

By now there was quite a puddle of gob on the floor and Krap carefully stepped out of it to stand on a dry piece of floor.

'But what would they do with a planet that has no vegetation?' asked Colin.

Krap shrugged his mighty shoulders, the muscles rippling as if they knew the answer but he did not. 'Who knows? Move on elsewhere? Destroy the galaxy?'

'And Worthing?' prompted Colin.

'Well yes, Worthing as well I suppose,' mused Krap. Then he took the cue and started to look a little brighter. 'Worthing, yes, subterfuge Librarian. I needed a cover story to be on Earth while I guarded the portal, so that I would not be found out by any of thine authorities. So did I start work in Ye City of London as something I believe thou wouldst call a stockbroker. No work to do and no suspicions cast on my ah, extraterrestrial habits. Indeed did I think that most of ye stockbrokers were not of this planet any more so than I.'

Colin nodded sagely in agreement.

'Anyway,' continued Krap, 'once did I oversleep on the wrong train home and did meet the Warrior of Worthing awaiting a happening at ye station. And yea, Librarian, did he regale me with such stories the like of which will go down the anus of history. Ah!'

Krap sighed and looked into the distance, a dreamy look on his face and a distinct moistness to his eyes. 'How can I forget that greeting,' he recalled tenderly, 'that "twentypee for a cup of tea mate", or "Gorblessya guv".'

Colin thought it tactful to change the subject. 'So how did you know about this?' he pointed to the skinned, congealing mess of dead beasties that was oozing out over the floor. Krap looked at Colin coquettishly and winked a massive bicep at him.

'We are entwined Librarian, thee and me. In thought and in mind. Sylvester knows it's hard sometimes, but I eliminate the trivial and respond to the obviously supernatural.' Colin felt sort of proud to know that somehow he and Krap were on the same wavelength. Yes, he thought, swelling with pride. Yes, that's good.

'So,' Krap went on, as he cracked his knuckles in a manly sort of way and pushed his glasses back up his nose whilst loosening his groin with a couple of swift knee-bends, 'When I saw the alarm in thine mind did I rush over from my rented flat across the road and ... well,' he grinned a superior and triumphant yet modest grin, 'thou knowest the rest.'

Krap then looked stern. 'But enough about me. Thou must think, Librarian, think. For 'tis foretold that there do be clues in the ancient scriptures. Why else would the beasts I have just done away with be looking to take the Chronicles away if not to hide the clues to heroes such as me? Why dost they have devilish monstrosities roaming the cosmos attempting to destroy all references to this fabled and mythical place except to allow the Gods of all animal matter to rule unaffected by heroic deed and create any sort of beast they wish, to smash the vegetable matter and crush it underfoot and eat it.'

Colin was stumped for a moment and not at all sure whether he should carry on with this or not. He turned to a comforting ditty in his head while he thought hard.

'Who is this Maria?' snapped Krap, mis-understanding. 'What problem does she pose? For by the might invested in me and my incredible bodily strength and power, shall I smite her with my trusty sword!'

Colin whimpered as the huge barbarian twirled his sword about his head, lost his grip and sent it spin-ning inches past Colin's head to land with a dull thud, point first, in the bookcase behind him.

Then he remembered. The shock had obviously loosened his brain as well as his bowels. His mind raced through the Chronicles. Footnote, really tiny italics, page 932, volume two. 'And yet forsooth for all ye who seek the fabled Isla St Clair, the first clue be the one-eyed snake-monster who be known as Snipe in the marshes beyond the village of B.'

'That's it!' cried Krap. He retrieved his sword and tucked it into his loin cloth. 'Away with me, Librar-ian. To Threa!'

As Colin rushed after Krap, past the festering yel-low body, an amazing and incredible thought hit him. He stopped dead in his tracks. Krap stopped too.

'What now Librarian? Do I sense thou wishest to relieve thineself?'

'No, no, just wait. Wait here a minute,' screeched Colin as he rushed off to the Library office. Incredible it may be, he thought, but perhaps ... perhaps ... He barged the door open; a startled Brian looked up from his audit sheets and snorted.

'Now then young Colin, what's the rush?' he whinged.

Rub your face in cockroach excrement and bugger off. 'Sorry Brian, won't be a sec,' and Colin shouldered the crush of Throbulets aside to rush to his desk and grab a shiny, orange paperweight. He clutched it to his heart for a moment, then peered closely at it. Set in a round, halfsphere of amber was what looked like a small brown kebab with small orange cubes stuck in it.

'I'm waiting, Colin,' droned Brian. He obviously expected an explanation.

Colin looked up. The excitement on his face was clear, and all he could garble was 'DNA ... DNA, Brian. Do you know what this means?'

'Of course, young Colin,' smarmed Brian as he leaned back in the chair. 'The National Dyslexic Association is renowned for its work with sufferers of the ailment. Why, I myself was a member for a good long while until I managed to conquer and control it. Hard to know, I appreciate.' He looked dreamily into the air, as if looking through the round window to the past. 'They used to send monthly newsletters, but I always found them sort of hard to read. Maybe that's why my membership lapsed. Still, back to work, har har, snort. No time for the past, eh young Colin.'

Colin ignored this and as he returned to where Krap stood, he felt all gooey and ecstatic. He looked hard at the object in his hands.

During his last adventure on Threa he had found a small turd clinging to his trouser-leg that he was sure he had passed some thirty-six hours after eating

Susan. Something in the back of his mind told him that it took thirty-six hours to process food through the body and out again, and so as a reminder of that beautiful girl he had once loved and then eaten, Colin had the turd set in amber and he kept it as a paperweight on his desk, because he was sure it contained a little bit of Susan.

His mind was now a tiz with thoughts of the DNA Accelerated Multiplier Unit that he and the mighty Krap had to find. Maybe – just maybe – he could use the vile machine to recreate Susan from his spoor, before destroying it.

The screen he had seen in the mental images obviously allowed tampering with the object to be recreated; hence the eight-legged chicken and, he supposed, the different sizes and colours of the Throbulets that had recently tried to borrow most of his books. Colin's imagination told him he could recreate Susan… but a Susan who LOVED COLIN. Truly, madly, deeply loved him. Oh God! Joy! Bliss!

Krap looked down at Colin as he approached and laughed. 'I see thou art excited by the quest ahead. Come, let us begone.'

Colin came, and ran rather stiffly after the Conqueror towards the Crime and Catastrophe Section, clutching the paperweight to his bosom and emitting little sobs of joy. He hardly had time to tuck it into his trouser pocket before he fell straight into a puddle of putrid, stinking water. He thrashed about a little then hauled himself to his feet and stared, open-mouthed, at the scene before him.

CHAPTER THREE

'A porpoise is like a dolphin but isn't spelt like one.'
Quote from Sylvester's *Chaos in the Underwater World*, which is yet
to be written.

He and the Conqueror, Colin was sure, were at the same place he had first encountered putrid, stinking Threan water. In the distance he could see the pens which held the jarfish and the stapilors. But where Krap's thatched waterhouse had once been there now stood the most amazing castle he had ever seen. Turrets and ramparts and flagpoles stuck out and reached for the clear blue sky. Pennants fluttered idly in the morning breeze. The huge drawbridge was down, massive chains either side, spanning the wide moat that appeared to go all the way round the castle.

Though a good mile away, the building was huge and it dominated the flat, desolate scenery. It was constructed of enormous grey blocks of nigtare, which Colin knew to be a compact, heavy, grey, knobbly sort of Threan stone, and there was not a soul in sight.

Nobody.

'Wow!' breathed Colin. 'Now that's what I call a waterhouse! How long have you had that?' He looked up at Krap, who for the first time ever stood stock-still. Not a muscle moved nor a tendon twitched. His mouth was slackly open as he, too, stared at the castle.

THREA

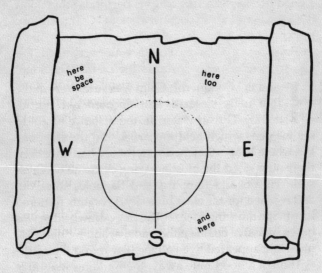

VIRTUAL REALITY

Plot Colin and his friends' adventures on this map of Threa,
which has been graciously donated by the Threan Walking
and Tourism board. Then set fire to its edges for added
authenticity.

The circle is a scale representation of the planet and the
directional vectors cross in a totally arbitrary or treeless
place thereupon.

This will bring the story to life and you will feel that you are
right there on Threa with Colin.

But do ask a grown-up to help you with the matches.

Colin was puzzled, but as he started to ask another question Krap twitched into action and, ripplingly, drew his broadsword. As he held it high above his head the blade gleamed in the sunlight and his muscles tightened with the strain. He opened his mouth and took a deep breath. His chest expanded by a good fifty centimetres and his pectorals strained at the bronzed skin. Expecting a shout, Colin still got rather a shock when it came.

'Build on my land, would you?' screamed the barbarian ferociously towards the castle. 'Desecrate the memory of my fabulous friends would you? Their bones are reclaimed by the soil but I shall not allow anyone to ... not to, ah ... No one shall build on their graves! For by everything that is Krap shall I not cease from mental strife, nor shall my sword sleep in my hand 'til we have unbuilt thine poxy castle stone by stone and hurled it away into thine faces. Aiiiieee!'

As Krap strode off towards the distant building Colin had to run to keep up. He had to admit that it was fair enough not to want anyone to build such structures on the graves of Kelvin the Abbot and Bruce of the Ledgers, Krap's two faithful friends who had been brutally murdered by the Thargs (who Colin and Krap had then eaten, as he recalled), but for anyone to claim they would pull this place down stone by stone was pushing it a bit. Colin was not sure he wanted any part of this.

He tried to calm the mighty Conqueror down as he strode ever nearer the castle, broadsword held directly out in front of him, as if threatening the very ground he walked on.

'Look, um Krap, um Mr Conqueror, sir, don't you

think we should, ah, at least just sort of think this thing over first? Just a little?'

Krap snarled and spat out of the corner of his mouth in disdain. The spittle slopped over his lower lip and dribbled down his chin. It dropped in thin, elastic strings onto his gleaming chest, and sent little bubble-filled globules racing down and to the side.

'Look,' reasoned Colin, who was by now out of breath and gasping slightly. 'Shouldn't we first at least talk to Waah?'

Krap sneered again. 'And who is Waah?' he asked, as he turned his head to look at Colin. 'Is he mightier or more knowledgeable than I, Krap the Invincible?' His steely gaze met thin air and he stopped to look behind him. Colin had tripped over and now lay flat on his front in another fetid little pool of water.

Krap let out a huge belly-laugh. 'Come, Librarian, for we near the structure that I have pledged to raze to the ground. Should I tolerate profanity of the worst kind and sacrilegious practices over the graves of mine friends?'

Colin got up and spat out the horrible, stinking water which had splashed into his mouth. He spat out the stringy bits which stayed on his tongue, and retched when he passed his tongue over the gritty bits and small, globule-like water-dwellers which stuck to his teeth. He took off his glasses to wipe them on his handkerchief; the dried snot scraped little lines across the lenses, but he put them back on and gasped in awe.

Somehow, during his fall, the castle had drawn closer, so that now he and Krap stood at the end of the drawbridge. Looking up they were dwarfed by the massive, cold lumps of nigtare that reached for the puffy small clouds that had started to gather in the sky. Looking down, they saw the huge moat full of brown, scummy water that seemed to writhe and churn with the movements of untold monstrosities.

Colin shuddered.

Krap started to stride across the wooden drawbridge and his cry echoed around the empty courtyards inside the mighty walls. 'Ho there, stand and face me o heathen scum. Be thou afraid of me who be Krap the mighty Conqueror, barbarian of extraordinary abilities?'

The walls stood eternally patient, throwing his voice back at him as Krap, followed by Colin, moved into the main area of the castle. Colin reckoned the enclosed bit to be about as big as three football pitches or two Clacton Libraries. The dirt floor was covered in gaily coloured tents of all shapes and sizes, flags fluttering in the breeze and awnings rippling like the sinewy curves of the barbarian's muscles.

Nothing moved except the flags and the awnings. Nobody answered. Suddenly a voice floated down, apparently from above them. It tinkled and chimed in an almost childish but camp sort of way, rather like the late Kenneth Williams, thought Colin.

'Now put that thing away and don't let's be silly,' it said.

Colin and Krap looked up as one to see three beings descending slowly through the air down the side of a large corner tower. They all three were dressed alike: tights bulging with masculinity, a bodice, and a large pair of wings attached to their backs. One figure was entirely green down to his short hair, eyes and teeth. One was similarly red,and the other blue. Each carried a foot-long wand with an appropriately coloured six-point star. Colin thought they sort of shimmered in the sunshine.

The three fairies (for indeed that is what they were) each alighted daintily on one foot, with the other cocked teasingly behind, and looked down on Colin then up at the mighty Krap, who was also immobilized by this vision.

'Hello,' cooed the red fairy to Colin. 'And welcome, oh One Of Mighty Intellect and Unusual Habits.' He surveyed Krap as one would a choice side of beef. 'And who are you, big boy?' he asked, flushing a deep crimson colour. Little beads of pink sweat broke out on his fairy forehead.

Krap recovered his composure and twirled his huge weapon before him then stopped it suddenly, held in a rock-like grip level with his chest a mere centimetre from the fairy's throat.

'I am Krap,' he threatened through clenched teeth. 'Conqueror of all and answerable to none. This is the Librarian as you doubtless know, and we are on a quest to destroy an abominable machine and protect thereby the Balance of Nature on this planet. Identify thineselves.'

The fairy looked at his blue colleague and pouted at him. His friend shrugged, and the red wand moved ever so slightly and touched the blade of Krap's sword. The weapon turned into a large feather duster and the fairies giggled.

'Now, now, let's not get off on the wrong foot shall we?' admonished Red gaily. 'We are the Faieries of Threa With The Twelve Cinh' – a Threan unit of measure almost equal to the Earth inch – 'Wands. This,' he twirled dramatically around, 'is our abode.

'I am Aphid Spivell, and he...' he pointed his wand

at the blue faierie, who threw up his hands in mock terror and then giggled, '... is Big Shanjee, and our green buddy here is Nerd Benkis.' Nerd Benkis curtseyed.

Colin gasped as Krap self-consciously tried to stuff his overlong feather duster into the waistband of his pink loin cloth.

'The Fairies of Threa!' Colin breathed in awe.

'No love, the FAIERIES of Threa,' corrected Aphid gently.

Colin's mind rushed through the *Chronicles of Ancient Threa* volume one, page 1037, footnote (iii). 'And lo, it was believed that there were maybe in the dim and distant past of this planet's history some faieries who inhabited parts of the planet but nobody is that old so nobody can be sure.'

'But, but ...' started Colin.

'Well,' said Aphid, who had obviously mind-read Colin's question. 'It's like this.' He put his weight onto one hip, folded an arm across his chest and rested the other elbow on it, gently rubbing his lips in slow, sensual circles with his fingers as he talked. 'Mummph munmph fummmuf.'

'Sorry?' asked Colin politely.

'I said,' Aphid snapped petulantly, removed the fingers from his mouth and then stamped lightly on the ground. A small circle of daisies immediately sprang up. 'I said, we were recreated by the Gods from our particles of essence and want to live here. OK?'

Colin's hand instinctively went to his pocket at the mention of the recreation and he reassuringly touched the amber paperweight. Soon, my love, soon, he thought with a tiny thrill.

'And,' said Nerd Benkis coyly, looking at Colin, 'we'd like you to live with us too.' He sighed deeply and blushed racing green. 'It's so long since we had any fun with our wands.'

Colin stepped back in horror. Thoughts flashed through his mind of being a sex-slave for eternity to these three ancient beings, for surely that was what they wanted. The fear dribbled out of his mind and down his trembling legs, and he looked pathetically at Krap. His eyes pleaded and his knees wobbled.

Just as the faieries read Colin's thoughts and started to smile smugly, Krap stopped fiddling with his duster and threw it angrily to the ground.

'Desist!' he cried. Everyone jumped. 'Enough!' he continued. 'We are on a quest and you will not deter us. Now return mine trusty broadsword and tell us the way to the one-eyed snake.'

'Now you're talking!' smarmed Aphid, as he turned the duster back into the shining soul-eater Krap called a sword. The other faieries fidgeted comfortably and they all went moist in the eyes. 'There's your sword, so come on upstairs big fella and we'll look for that old one-eyed snake, shall we?' Aphid was by now burgundy in the face.

Krap bent down to pick up the sword, and in the same movement sent Aphid Spivell's head spinning from his shoulders and bouncing across the ground. Blood gushed from the empty neck and the body slumped down in a heap.

Colin jumped at the sight of sudden death as Nerd Benkis' body was run through by Krap's blade, and the barbarian's battle-cry erupted from his thoat. Krap advanced menacingly towards Big Shanjee, who had turned white with a hint of blue and who stood, trembling with fear and disgust at the sight of his dead brothers. He seemed incapable of movement. Colin knew what was coming and couldn't look. He turned away as Krap swung whilst grimly repeating the phrase, 'Build on my friends would you?' over and over again.

A soft squelch with a crunch in the middle told Colin it was over. He looked around and was hit full in the face by the bodiless head of Big Shanjee. As he launched himself down the ramp of unconsciousness he barely heard Krap apologize.

Neither did he hear the weak, plaintive cry for help that drifted upwards· on the light breeze from the dungeons below. But Krap did. (Colin would find this out later, as he was obviously, at this stage, not capable of knowing it, so while this piece is slightly out of context on a time basis, it is as it appears in the authorized Saga.)

CHAPTER FOUR

'And there's Absolute Chaos on the pitch!'
Twad Veanos commentating on the 1987 Throbuletball
Association cup final. Final result as follows:
Kotestrent .... 2 (scorers Krap 23 Spasmo 47)
Absolute Chaos .... don't know.

Meanwhile Yoof, one of the twin Gods of Vegetation, had felt forced to change his name to Untilatelyoof, and his brother had changed his name from Untilatelyoof to Yoof. To complete their disguises, so that they might escape the tyranny and repression of the Bestial Gods and their Blue Peter Cult, they both grew even longer beards and moved to a place in the country.

Unfortunately, they discovered that their chosen place of exile, the Isla St Clair on the Vitamin Sea, just happened to be the historical homeland of the Thargs, recently recreated by the Bestial Gods' monstrous machine. So the Yoof twins were forced to hide from Tharg and Bestial God alike, who moved with the Thargs so that they could help guard the dreadful machine. The Yoof twins were trapped. There was no way of escape without being spotted and set-upon.

Untilatelyoof had taken to his bed, which was woven of living reeds and grass. Yoof, at the entrance to their foliage den, sighed heavily as he surveyed the limited horizon of their island prison. Untilatelyoof stirred and weakly asked, 'What news, brother mine?'

Yoof just looked tenderly at his brother and sighed

wistfully. Untilatelyoof laid his head back on the pillow of living fungus, and rolled his eyes up wearily. 'Oh brother,' he moaned, 'my strength is yet weak from the efforts of sending that "once-in-a-green-moon celestial peak-time inter-galactic time-travelling cross-over facsimile" to our champion on Earth.'

Yoof at once sat down on the edge of the bed and started gently to rub his brow. Then he did the same to his brother's brow. 'Oh yes,' he murmured in reply, ''twas indeed fortunate that thou wert able to cross galaxies and space with our message to our Gateway Guardian for to call him to our aid and rid us of this dastardly machine. For now is the problem so bad that needs must we have his aid.' He looked down at his brother fondly. ''Tis also fortunate that thou shalt not be called upon to do so again for another 100,000 Ages.' (Note here that an Age is equivalent to the life-cycle of the Threan Spider-Plant, which is generally about six Earth years with careful watering or 6.3 years with no attention paid to it whatsoever.) 'For 'tis then the next green moon.'

Untilatelyoof stood, with difficulty, then sunk back into the bed.

'And what news of our Krap, oh caring twin?'

Yoof took a deep breath. His eyes betrayed his deep concern. 'Thine stools are still little improved, brother. Mine are, as ever, green.'

'Is he abroad, our Conqueror?' asked Untilatelyoof, wheezily ignoring his brother's crack.

'Nay,' came the reply, 'I have word he is here on the planet with one of great intellect and little physical prowess. The grasses report that the energy patterns and footprints are familiar from another time. It bodes well but we must await their arrival, should they be able to get here.

'But meanwhile I have received news that our collection of Michaelmouse Daisies has been decimated in Southern Threa by a herd of dinosaurs created by "those others,"' he said this with venom, 'and our yellow Margerinemugs have been virtually obliterated by roving herds of big game animals.'

'And the exquisite clumps of Remember-You-Yesses we created and planted our very selves near our former home?' asked Untilatelyoof hopefully.

Yoof shook his head sadly, and merely said, 'Our Scruffygiraffes too. All gone. But fear not, brother mine, for Krap the Mighty Conqueror must surely be close-by this Island.'

Any hope that had entered Yoof's voice scorched out of the fire-exit with the realization that there was an enchantment placed upon the Isla St Clair by the Ancient Thargs. This meant that the place could only be found by following a complex series of contacts and clues throughout the planet. They themselves had stumbled across it by sheer chance and a lot of God-awful luck.

Just then a wandering Tharg sentry stuck his heads into the twin Gods' parlour. Two heads looked curiously about and two mouths fell wide open on seeing the brothers sat beside each other on the bed. Here were the two murderers that the sergeant had told them about. They were worth two months home leave and seventy spondus a month for life. As the Tharg had been recently genetically recreated the home leave was not much use to him, but the money would come in handy.

But before the beast could run and raise the alarm,

the creepers which ringed the rude doorway to the secret hideout were activated by Untilatelyoof, stirred into action by the intrusion though still desperately short of strength. The Tharg was quickly encircled, and speeding lengths of vine wrapped themselves around his necks before he could let out any sound. The body twitched and spasmed for a few minutes, then slumped lifeless to the floor.

Yoof attacked the corpse with Gusto, his trusty pen-knife, hacking off a limb for himself and draining a cup of blood for his brother, whose alimentary tracts were not yet up to the full digestion of meat.

'These infrequent visitors bring much needed sustenance,' said Yoof as he chewed the carrion (for these Gods of Vegetation could eat nought but meat, having foresaken all vegetable matter because, having made the stuff, they felt responsible for it.) 'However, we needs must be careful to remain hidden for our own safety until we can find a way off this accursed island or destroy the wretched machine, or hopefully both.'

Untilatelyoof stirred his plasma thoughtfully. 'Mayhap, brother mine, there be a way of speeding the arrival of the Champion and his accomplice to destroy the accursed Blue Peter Advent Crown or whatever they call the infernal thing.'

Yoof took the half-chewed limb from his mouth and looked quizzical. 'How so brother?' he asked.

'Create a path of waving vegetation, brother mine, a swathe of moving plants, no more than thirteen ginks wide.' (Editorial note. 'Gink' is an Ancient Threan God measure of length equal to the size of a God's appendage. There was great variation in the actual measure, especially during times of great excitement, and the rule was long ago abandoned by all but the most Godly. Being twins, the Yoofs could generally agree on the length of a gink, and so continued to use it as a rule.) 'This path to be between us and the travellers. It would take no more to guide them here.'

Yoof nearly choked with the excitement. Immediately thirteen ginks seemed a more daunting prospect, but the plan was sound.

'Yes, yes,' he spluttered, 'a veritable host of movement shall surely speed their journey here! I shall instruct the flora accordingly.'

'Well done brother. Let us be praised.'

CHAPTER FIVE

Therefore, ERGO is an anagram of GORE.
The first sentence of 'Foundations of Chaos', an essay by Sylvester,
aged 10.

When Colin came to, he was bouncing heavily on the shoulders of Krap as the Conqueror strode mightily through some sort of forest. Every step taken by the huge barbarian ended in a squelch and a squeak as the pink loin cloth dried out, and this was quickly followed by Colin being thrown into the air, to be hauled down by his extremities, once more firmly meeting Krap's muscle-bound, iron-hard shoulders.

Colin tried to speak so that Krap would know he was OK now and put him down, but every time he gathered his breath the Conqueror took another stride, and 'Ooof' was the only noise Colin could make as he became re-acquainted belly-first with those oak-like shoulders.

Eventually Krap stopped and promptly shrugged Colin to the ground. He looked around, apparently surprised by Colin's groaning, and his face creased into a wide grin.

'Hah! Librarian! Forgive me, but I became so used to you being on my back that I quite forgot where I was!' His eyes glazed over behind the wire-rimmed specs, as had Colin's. 'Yeay, Librarian,' sighed Krap, 'did I think myself yomping once more through the deserts of Northern Threa, mine pack on my back and my trusty broadsword by my side.

'Ye Gods, but those were good days! My only companions were Hope, Faith and a female sheep called Gladys ...' he tailed off into silence and dropped back into reality. 'Art ready Librarian?' he asked gruffly.

Colin got up tenderly and gently rubbed his trousers down. As he felt the cold, wet patches of cloth he suddenly remembered Susan, and his hand shot into his pocket. Relief!

The paperweight was still there. Smooth, polished and ... and almost vibrating with anticipation. Colin quickly put his other hand into his other pocket and self-consciously tried to arrange himself so that it was not too obvious.

'Um yes,' he responded, drawing his jacket closer around him. 'I er think I'm ready. Ah, off we go then.'

Krap guffawed and turned to go. Colin heard a noise next to them and looked to his side. His mouth dropped open and he drooled. He went limp everywhere except in the loin region. He was in love, and Susan was forgotten.

She stood a couple of metres from Colin and had obviously been jogging alongside the Conqueror for some time. A light sheen of sweat covered her bronzed, shiny skin. Her beautiful, firm breasts, which swelled like smooth footballs above her brief bikini top, gently moved up and down, up and down, up and down as she controlled her heavy breathing. There wasn't an ounce of spare fat on her and her muscles were firm, and sleek, and rippling without being too obvious, giving her six-foot curvy frame the image of a well-groomed, top flight racehorse.

She wore a tiny pair of matching gold bikini bottoms and Colin could see that either she was very, very good at jigsaws and stencil work or else she was that gorgeous brown colour all over her body!

As he wondered about what was under those miniscule pieces of cloth, Colin looked up at her face and his heart actually stopped (though not for long; it was probably just that he suddenly became aware of the deep, invasive throbbing going on around his body and the few microseconds between beats just seemed like a long time in the presence of this goddess). Sparkling blue eyes, crystal clear like the water running through a mountain brook, looked at him; not directly into his eyes but just below, in a submissive 'I'll do anything to please you big boy' sort of way. Long blond eyelashes flickered slightly and her full, red lips pouted, then parted smoothly as if to speak. But instead she slowly licked her perfect white teeth and those ruby lips with the very tip of her tongue, as if daring Colin to say something first.

Long, silky blond hair framed this vision's face and shoulders; the sun shone down and made it seem as if the Gods had made perfection and placed a golden halo around this beauty of beauties, this ravishing, full-breasted, smooth-hipped sex machine who, right now, looked as if she fancied Colin.

Krap laughed as he read the thoughts that rushed from Colin's mind to his inter-leg region.

'She is called Norah,' he boomed, 'Norah Spleens. I rescued this fair maid at the castle, whilst thou did sleep the sleep of the sleepy.'

'Wh ... wh ... what was she um doing there?' squeaked Colin. He could barely talk, and certainly couldn't think straight nor tear his gaze from this gorgeous creature. Norah smiled nervously and looked down at the ground, blushing slightly. She held her hands together behind her back, which only served to accentuate her feminine charms at the front. Colin was on the point of bursting forth and doing God only knows what; he wanted to stroke her skin, to run trembling fingers through her silken hair, to bury his head forever between those smooth, smooth thighs, but most of all he wanted her to . . .

'She is from the Syorks tribe of warrior women, who are renowned for their beauty and ferocity,' interrupted Krap. 'But she was enslaven by those faieries,' he spat, remembering his recent victims, 'and programmed forever to respond to the desires of males. Thus could they keep themselves amused watching her perform the most hideous deeds at their behest and with a variety of beasts. This, Librarian, would have been your fate also, had thee been taken by surprise.'

Colin shuddered. 'She'll obey *any* male?' he asked, still slack-jawed but starting to piece the puzzle together. He continued to stare at Norah, who giggled demurely and looked down at her beautiful feet. Her breasts rolled gently like oil on the water.

'Aye, Librarian,' answered Krap seriously, 'for have I earlier tested this for our own safety, and indeed did she do all manner of things to me in mine furs which I did devise as a test for better knowledge of this abominable curse.' His eyes glossed slightly, and he murmured, 'She passed the strictest of tests, yes she did,' in a faraway voice.

Colin looked at Krap, and at the glaze in his eyes. He suddenly hated Krap more than anything in the whole world. Or any other world. Colin turned swiftly to Norah who looked at him shyly.

'Is this true?' he demanded. 'Did those faieries enchant you in this way? Do you have to obey the commands of any male and serve him accordingly?'

She nodded sadly, then licked her lips ever so gently.

'What, even me?' asked Colin fearfully. There. He'd said it. He waited for rejection. But Norah nodded the affirmative again, and looked Colin full in the eye. She pushed her hands up her back and unclipped something ... Oh My God, her bra fell to the floor and Colin gasped at the two huge, soft, firm, warm, bronzed, nippled ... Oh No, he screeched in his head, and he never noticed Krap disappear in search of firewood, obviously not interested in the proceedings.

Norah walked towards Colin now, holding his stare with those magical eyes. She managed to appear tough, yet oh so soft, all at the same time. Her breasts swayed gently as she moved, and Colin caught the scent of something familiar as she approached, though his mind was too scrambled to identify it beyond the generalities of the fish family.

Then she stood before him, towering over him, a whole mountainful of yielding woman, breasts at his face level. Norah cupped one firm, full bosom in her hand, lifted it slightly, and with the other hand pulled Colin's face forward towards the proffered gift; that wondrous golden orb.

Colin's mind hit meltdown, and as he closed his eyes he shuddered violently and exploded further down. Ignoring the wetness of his groin area he stuck out his tongue to lick Norah; he smelt that smell again and licked her, and she tasted of succulent tomatoes, and ripe cheese, and garlic, and that smell ... anchovies! and ... he opened his eyes and saw that he gripped a large, deep-pan pizza between his teeth that dripped cheese and tomato and anchovies. He looked about in horror, but couldn't see Norah anywhere.

At that moment Krap returned, and started to guffaw with side-splitting laughter. 'I told thee, oh early one, she be bewitched. For the Syorks tribe be also shape-changers. As she is now an enchantress doomed to pursue male pleasure she must satisfy the most urgent desire, then move on to the next one, though her eternal damnation be never to be satisfied herself.'

The Conqueror could see the confusion still on Colin's face, so he started to explain once more, very slowly and carefully. 'The height of human male pleasure and sexual desire be ejaculation, Librarian. Can I make an assumption here and say that thou hast 'come' in the last few seconds?' Colin nodded in miserable agreement. He was too upset to be embarrassed.

'Thus,' continued Krap as if to a child, 'Norah doth believe your first and strongest desire, that of sexual play, to be fulfilled, as thou hast filled thine loin cloth with the evidence. Hence she hast moved to fulfill thine next strongest desire which, obviously, was hunger. This she has done by shape-changing and selflessly allowing thee to eat her. The whole process be automatically controlled by the enchantment, which cannot be revoked without the original enchanter, and that be now impossible.'

As the pizza slowly slid from his lips and gradually changed back into a stunning, pouting Norah who seemed to be no worse the wear for her experience,

Colin's eyes misted over and he started to cry. Huge, gasping sobs of despair came from his mouth. He had found the girl of his dreams. A girl so beautiful, so perfect that she only had to walk up to him (admittedly with no top on) and he would make a bucketful of mess in his trousers. Then she'd turn into a jacket potato, or a bloody mug of cocoa or something. And he could never, never get to touch her, or feel her, or roll about with her and point out the stars and laugh together and ...

And he cried and cried and cried. He vaguely saw, through the veil of salt water before his eyes, Krap slinking off into the undergrowth with Norah. Her hands seemed suspiciously stuffed down the front of Krap's loin cloth, as if searching for one she'd made earlier.

'Wait,' shouted Colin.

Krap turned. Norah continued with her search. 'What is it?' he cried, with a smile on his face. 'We have no time for self-indulgence. We must away. The one-eyed snake-monster thing awaits! Then must we away to seek Snipe.'

'No, no,' gasped Colin as he struggled to control his sobbing. 'What's that noise?'

Above the deathly hush of the forest and his tinnitus and his crying, Colin had caught the noise. Like a furious wind, he thought. It was pleading, and crackling and, most important of all, coming towards them.

Suddenly, and as if by magic, the forest before them erupted into action. Trees, shrubs and bushes started to wave maniacally around, though Colin could feel no wind. He looked wildly about and noticed that behind them, and to the sides, the vegetation was still. Only a narrow band of foliage was active in front of the travellers, though it disappeared to the horizon.

Krap noticed the same. 'What enchantment is this?' he yelled above the rustling and crackling that was now very loud indeed.

Strangely, Colin's fear reminded him how hungry he was and he sank to his knees with weakness as the pain clawed at his belly and lightened his sphincter. He almost regretted not eating the Norah-pizza now, and that thought made him feel even worse. Krap pulled free his broadsword and the keen blade sliced clean through the loin cloth which fell to the floor. Norah quickly let go of whatever it was she had a hold of, and was pushed away to hide in the bushes, with the command from Krap, 'Go hide in the bushes, wench, until I have need of thee.'

Colin barely had time to marvel at the firm, rippling buttocks and the tiny thingy before Krap set about the flora with a brutality that was awesome to behold. His sword ripped through branches and treetrunks. Bushes were rent assunder and sent flying; grass was trampled underfoot and wood splinters flew everywhere. In Krap's fury he hacked large conifers into tiny match-stick sized pieces.

Sawdust clogged Colin's eyes momentarily and he mechanically removed his glasses to wipe them. He was totally gobsmacked by the barbarian's performance. And then, as suddenly as it had started, the noise ceased and the forest once more fell still and silent. Krap's sword was poised just inches from a rather sweet flowering cherry, about to slice it in twain, when he stopped and looked about at the tranquility. Shattered stumps and strips of wood lay everywhere in a five-metre radius. Saplings lay bent double, the sap bleeding from their slashed trunks and branches. Bushes were ripped up and ground into the, er, ground, and smaller plants were crushed beyond recognition.

The foliage had decided that it didn't mind being trodden on a bit, nor brushed against occasionally, or even sometimes losing some of its fruit to a lonely passing traveller. But if the Gods wanted it to be cut to buggery and back that was just not on. Vegetable matter was all for an easy life; there was precious little of it around anyway, without letting some muscle-bound barbarian hack it about.

Krap signalled alarm, and Colin looked over in the direction of Krap's stare. In the distance, through the shattered foliage, they saw three bright lights standing out against the gathering gloom. One was pink, one purple and one orange.

Colin warily followed Krap, who advanced on the lights slowly and carefully with his sword held out in front of him. Colin made out the three luminous shapes of brightly coloured faieries – just like the ones they had met on the site of Krap's waterhouse, and ... yes ... now Colin understood what that strange yellow creature in the library had been! A faierie!

That footnote had warranted no more than four lines in the Chronicles, thought Colin, and yet now they had encountered faierie-folk of red and yellow and pink and green, purple and orange and blue!

A tune tripped over Colin's mind but it failed to get up as they walked slowly towards the three gaily coloured mystic folk.

'I shall deal with these before they have a chance to use their magic,' growled Krap, as he held his blade in the two-handed 'cleave-thine-enemy-in-twain' grip he had perfected in his many years of barbarianism.

The faieries stood still on a small hillock, watching the travellers approach.

'Hail,' hailed the pink one. 'Who art thou? For are we the Faieries of Threa and this be our domain. This hillock be where we camp.' He dropped a wrist and minced around his companions for a moment to much giggling and merriment.

'We wouldst know thine names. Big boy.' This last was a pointed comment to Krap, who started to growl menacingly.

'I am Krap,' he rumbled. 'Conqueror of all. And shall I slay thee before thee can use thine magic as did thine friends who did perish before thee?' His voice rose in a crescendo, and the ensuing silence was deafening.

As Krap advanced, oblivious to the hanging back of Colin and Norah, the orange faierie pointed almost casually at Krap who froze in mid-stride, poised to take a step, and unable to move. The orange faierie turned to his companions.

'Did you hear that, Purple, heart? There are more like us! Could it be?'

Purple touched Orange playfully on the shoulder and turned him a sort of puce colour which annoyed him. As Orange struggled to regain his colour, Purple questioned Colin.

'Who are these colleagues of ours?' he asked. 'What, ah, colours?' as he licked his pearly purple teeth.

'Well, um, well, there was a ... a ... yellow one ah, in the library ...' started Colin.

Purple turned to his friends, both of whom stood splendid in their original colours once more. They both had their hands firmly planted on their hips.

'Blow me!' said Purple. Orange and Pink fell to

their knees before him in mock acceptance. 'Dough Patsy! So he's still around somewhere eh? I would so like to get in touch.'

Colin felt it prudent not to mention the fact that Dough Patsy had been hewn limb from limb by Krap, so he hummed a little song to himself nervously in case the faieries could read minds.

They could.

'You bitch,' exclaimed Purple, thrusting an accusing finger and his hips at Colin. 'Yes, Dough is a dear but he could never fall for you, love. Too damned common. How dare you.'

Colin was struck stiff and found he couldn't move. He could see, he could hear, but he couldn't move a muscle.

As the faieries tripped down the hillock towards him, eyeing his groin region with something approaching hunger, Colin grew increasingly worried. What he needed now was Krap the Conqueror to be there to save him, not prostrate in a walking position some two metres from him.

Immediately Norah turned into a hairy-arsed barbarian with a massive broadsword and dripping pink loin cloth, and smote the faieries soundly with a few mighty strokes. Their cries of masochistic ecstasy died with them as their bodies poured coloured blood over the grass. Krap got up, Norah returned to her normal beautiful self, and the companions moved off with little said amongst them. Colin watched with some regret the colours melt into each other to turn the ground a horrible brown colour. The faierie lights went out with a 'poof' as the travellers left the area behind.

*

53

Sometime later, as the trio trudged on through the woods, the air was filled with a loud, throbbing noise. The clearing was plunged into semi-darkness, as if a great shadow passed over the ground, and the noise increased in intensity until Colin could no longer bear it. He clamped his hands to his ears but the drone pumped through them, vibrating him to his very core. He saw Krap standing, open-mouthed, looking up at the sky apparently unruffled by the sound waves which pummelled Colin to his knees.

And then the noise stopped, abruptly and without warning. Daylight returned and Colin found his face was scrunched up tight against the barrier. He slowly relaxed his eyes and opened them. He could still feel that horrible, muffling pressure on the sides of his head and Krap's words were indistinct.

'What?' cried Colin.

'I said take thine hands from over thine ears,' yelled Krap from a few inches away. 'We have company.'

Dropping his hands to his sides Colin found the pressure gone, and his restored hearing sensed a light, tingling sound reverberating around the devastated clearing in which they still stood. In sheer astonishment he watched as the tingling manifested itself into lots of little lights which grew in intensity to form the outline of two people. The features filled in, and there before the travellers stood two men.

Colin was stunned.

Two men, who looked exactly like a couple of blokes who would boldly go where no man had gone before, had just materialized before him! Incredible! As if they had just beamed down from the ether or the ozone layer or outer space or something!

Colin could think of absolutely nothing to say,

although there was so much he wanted to ask, but Krap swung readily into action. He grasped the handle of his mighty weapon and held the blade high above his head.

'Who art thou?' he growled, threatening to cleave them in two with one mighty blow if the answer was in the slightest unsatisfactory.

The sort-of-in-charge-type-being looked cooly at Krap, then over to Colin. 'Niloc?' he queried.

Krap looked at Colin, puzzled. 'What is this Librarian? What language does this one speak? What demons are these?'

Colin started to say he didn't know then stopped. A realization of blinding clarity shot through his scrambled mind and he became excited and twitchy.

'No, no,' he raised a hand towards Krap's sap-covered blade. 'Wait.' He strode confidently forward. 'I think I can handle this. Niloc is Colin backwards. Leave it to me.'

He stopped a metre short of the two materialists and raised one hand in a Vulcan salute.

'Sey!' he spoke confidently.

'Say what?' asked the leader-type chap.

'What says he?' queried Krap who had lowered his blade and was wiping his glasses with a dock-leaf. He suddenly realized that he was still naked, and hurriedly tried to repair his loin cloth with loose staples while hiding behind a shattered tree-stump. Colin saw a slim, female arm writhe up to help him from behind the stump, and his agonized mind thought again of Norah; his lovely, perfect, wonderful, untouchable Norah. He bit his lip and fought back the tears as Krap fought off the arm.

'Um ...' started Colin, returning to the conversation, 'he says, uh, "Yes tow", I think.'

'Tow?' bellowed Krap who emerged from behind the stump with a newly patched-together nether-region-cover. 'What sorcery is this? That is my cousin's dog's name!' He turned to the two strangers who still had not moved. 'How knowest thou of this?' he threatened. His muscles rippled menacingly, as if he was barely able to keep control of his fighting instinct.

'Look,' said the captain-like person 'Let's start again. Are you,' he pointed at Colin, 'Niloc?'

Colin started to try and figure out what 'Cool, stel trats niaga' meant when he realized that the man was actually speaking English.

'Oh!' he cried aloud. 'Ah, yes, I suppose I am. Colin that is. Um, Niloc.'

'I,' said the alien, 'am Slogg, Captain of the Extra-Galactic Time-travelling Police Ship The Free Trade Zone. This is Chief Engineer Mee, and this,' he indicated the empty space to his left, 'is First Officer Incarter.'

Krap looked on, puzzled, but Colin was thrilled. 'He's invisible, isn't he? Incarter's invisible!'

Captain Slogg looked around, and then looked at Mee. Mee pointed silently upwards and four pairs of eyes saw two arms and two legs waving wildly out of a solid beech tree trunk some ten metres above the ground.

Slogg opened his communicator.

'Slogg to Free Trade Zone. You've beamed Incarter into a bloody tree, you idiots. Now get him back to the ship and fix him up. Pronto.'

Over the communicator Colin and the others heard

a muffled cry of ululation, which sounded like 'Uhurahurahurahuraaaaa!' and then a clearer voice came on. It reminded Colin of a cheeky chirpy Cockney-sparrow-type of person.

'Sorry, Captain, the Chief Beaming Officer just grabbed a packet of Scotties from a travel-pack and rushed down the apples and pears to the toilet cubicle for a phaser bank, sir. But don't worry sir, I'll do it sir. Cor, strike a light me old china plate, ready to energize sir.'

Slogg looked at Colin with a pained expression in his eyes as the arms, legs and a section of the tree trunk disappeared in a spangle of bright points of light. The top of the tree, freed from support by the removal of Incarter's section of trunk, crashed down onto Mee and crushed him.

Slogg snapped open his communicator once more. 'Listen, you gits, beam Mee up at once.'

The Captain disappeared then reappeared and then Mee and a further section of trunk spangled off into the ether. Slogg muttered something that sounded very like 'bleeding imbeciles,' and then turned to Colin, as if about to give a speech.

'I have two injured officers on board my vessel so I shall make this brief, Niloc. We come from the future. Two hundred years hence the entire galaxy is at peace under the benign leadership of one Niloc VI, who is the person solely responsible for peace throughout known space and within every known community, and who has single-handedly eradicated crime and taxes and single-motherhood.

'Without him man would not stand with man, nor man with beast nor woman with both in peace and harmony. He is the thread which binds together our very fabric of niceness and loveliness.

'However, an alien life-force from outside our galaxy, which refuses to renounce the ways of war and violence, has sent one of its own creations to destroy this leadership and probably take over our entire civilization as we know it today.'

Krap was obviously not a little confused by all this; indeed he seemed a lot confused by it, and Colin had to admit that he was unsure of where it was all headed. However, he did have a sneaking suspicion that he wasn't going to like it.

'The one they have sent,' continued Captain Slogg, 'is part man, part machine, part solid unthinking matter. It has the ability to move through time and space and has decided, according to our spies, on a course of action that threatens the very fabric and foundation of our worlds and beyond.

'It is the fourth in the series, constructed solely for this purpose; we have so far been fortunate in destroying the first three, but this one is so much more advanced that we have had difficulty tracking it.'

'What, you mean like Terminator?' asked Colin. He thought he was getting to grips with this and definitely didn't like what he heard.

'I know no Terminator,' answered Slogg, 'but this ... this monster is deadly efficient and is thus known as Terminal, as everything that it comes across tends to die. Terminal Four, to give it its correct title and sequence number.

'It has, we believe, traced Niloc VI's ancestry, and is at this very moment in time heading for this planet at this time-phase to destroy the very start of the Niloc lineage.'

Colin got a familiar squishy feeling in his stomach,

and started to tremble. 'So this Terminal Four is going to kill me?' he asked bluntly.

'It is programmed to eradicate the first in the line of Nilocs, and has a 99.9 per cent certainty of success,' said Slogg helpfully. 'It cannot get near Niloc VI for our protection and Guardian systems, and so it has chosen the past as its battleground.'

Colin collapsed in a stinking heap and started to sob uncontrollably. There was no place for the thought that he was supposed to father the ultimate Galactic leader of men. He just couldn't help but concentrate on the fact that Terminal Four was apparently certain to kill him first. Even the polished touch of the paperweight in his pocket brought no more than a limp reaction to him.

'No!' yelled Krap and everyone jumped. 'I shall not allow it!'

Colin immediately felt a little better, such was his faith in the mighty barbarian, and started to thank Krap between the tears.

'Not until we are done with our quest, anyway,' added Krap. Colin collapsed once more, the temporary reprieve all the worse for being so short lived.

'Anyway,' said Slogg as he opened his communicator, 'we will try and intercept him but we don't really know what Terminal Four looks like so it could be difficult. Now you must excuse me as I have some photon torpedoes to get rid of and the toilet paper on my ship is exceedingly soft. Good luck.' And he vanished.

Colin was a gibbering wreck, with more bodily orifices open than he should have, when Krap hauled him to his feet.

'Do not worry, Librarian, for this Terminal Four

being cannot hurt thee.'

'Whachameen?' slobbered Colin.

'Why if you were to die now then there would be no reason for Captain Slogg to visit us from the future, would there? Ergo you do not die.'

Ever so slowly, the logic permeated Colin's brain and he started to pull himself together. Krap was right. He couldn't die, otherwise the future would be changed and Slogg wouldn't come back to him, but he had, so that must be right. Feeling a little brighter, but still with that chilly feeling of being watched, or rather hunted, Colin got to his feet.

'Of course that's just one future that attaches itself to this particular strand of the present,' mused Krap quietly and almost to himself. 'It could be changed to run a parallel course, I suppose. There are, after all, parallel dimensions and 759 parallel worlds. So it could happen.'

But Colin wasn't listening. He was looking warily about for Terminal Four whilst trying to rearrange his sodden trousers. Norah appeared from her hiding place looking as gorgeous and sexy as ever, and Colin started to melt once more. She was fully dressed in her bikini now, and that silky, sexy walk of hers started his excitement anew. He had to look away and decided to have as little to do with her as possible.

Somewhere in the middle of a desert on the other side of the planet, unheard by anyone and unseen by others, a British Airways Club Class check-in desk for Paris, complete with frustrated queue and the git at the front who won't believe he's in the wrong airport, briefly shimmered in the twilight, then disappeared. Or did it?

Nobody knows for sure.

CHAPTER SIX

An enlarged Protestant can be painful and may require minor surgery.
From Sylvester's bestselling *Why Other Religions are All Crap*.

Yoof, at the window, gazed wistfully out across the woodland and sub-tropical areas of the Isla St Clair. He looked at the path of vegetation that waved and shook as if in a storm, although there was no sign of wind.

Untilatelyoof stood next to him, also looking out wistfully. 'That wist in a mornay sauce was excellent repast, brother dearest, and be I verily now full of it. For tea I believe that rat or vole pie would suffice,' he said dreamily, remembering the meal that had stuffed them full not so very long ago.

Yoof tried to vocalize something that had been concerning him for a few minutes now. 'Dost not think, oh twin, that by the very nature of our signal, which is destined to bring the Champion to our very door, others should also us be able to find? H'mm?'

Untilatelyoof stared at his brother and was about to ask him what he had been smoking when he suddenly understood.

'Art correct in thine presumption blood-relation mine. Others mayhap shall possibly be in a position to discover us due to our guidance path, which is to guide to us and towards our general ... yes, yes, you're right.'

With a wave of his hand, which gave just the right representation of a palm frond flapping idly in the wind, Untilatelyoof attracted the attention of the nearest medium-sized fruit-bearing bush that he knew would have roots deep and wide enough to be able to spread the gospel that he was about to issue forthwith.

'One thousand ginks,' he mumbled. The concentration poured out of his brow in tiny droplets of perspiration. 'One thousand ginks from this here hidey-hole shalt stop waving immediately so that we may not be spotted and undone. This shall still bring the mighty one close enough to find us.'

A thousand ginks-worth of vegetation stopped its furious flapping and curled up its flowers for a rest. Out of sight of the Gods, a narrow patch of vegetation some thirteen ginks wide and one gink long was all that remained of their path.

Untilatelyoof stirred beside his brother and suddenly doubled up with a desperate cry. 'Oh mine belly! Mine belly!' he cried in obvious agony.

Yoof at once helped him to the bed. ''Tis thine karma, twin,' he soothed as if there was nothing to do but wait it out.

'Oh ye God, who is omnipresent and most high and created all including us and our powers, is it so?' wailed Untilatelyoof. 'Is it my karma, my pre-destination to be so pained for the rest of mine eternal lifetime?'

Yoof looked peeved. 'No brother, I meant not karma but korma, that chicken korma from last night, for that it is that does so react. For earlier today did I need to spend mine prayer-time on the celestial toilet talking to God, and did mine stools tell to me that 'twas the korma from yesterday. For you know 'tis a gift I have, twin.'

'You mean you're talking crap,' gasped Untilatelyoof, who breathed a little easier now.

'I am not, forsooth, thou knowest it to be true,' snapped his brother.

Untilatelyoof stood and stumbled to the window once more, still clutching his belly. 'Krap, brother,' he said.

'No, no, 'tis true and verily do you ken it,' cried Yoof.

'Nay, I mean crap ... Krap ... 'tis a sign! Our hero approaches, surely, and we must ensure guidance here.' He stared hard at his brother.

'You must send the Cunningham.'

Untilatelyoof gasped. 'Not ... the Cunningham?'

Yoof stood his ground. 'Yeay brother, 'tis time. We must activate the beast for must we use all means at our disposal to ensure the safe arrival of our saviours.'

In a swamp some miles away a huge, gnarled mango tree pulled its massive roots from the shallow swamp bed and set off to find Krap in response to its masters' wishes. It stood some thirty ginks in circumference and some three hundred ginks high.

It was named Cunningham after a particularly big bloke who had studied with Yoof at the Celestial College of Concentrated Clairvoyance and Catastrophies; Bestial Annihilation (Big Stuff) Course. However, whereas Yoof had finished the course, achieving a very respectable 74 per cent in the final exam, Cunningham had dropped out after the first millenium and gone to programme computers in Kotestrent. It was a tough job, or an easy one, depending on how you looked at it, because computers had not yet been invented on Threa – but that was just the kind of bloke Cunningham was.

Yoof was so nervous that he unknowingly created a small, blue, tear-shaped flower, which would be known, in years to come, as Gods' Misery. In about three thousand years' time, it would strangely mutate and start to kill all the priests it could find for no reason.

CHAPTER SEVEN

'Did you say, something?'
From Sylvester's bestseller *The God Out There.*

As the adventurers trudged on through Nappy Valley and out onto the pampers plains of Threa, Colin's lust for a re-created Susan took a definite second place in his mind to the fact that Terminal Four was trying to kill him, but even that was not as important to him as trying to find a way of having sex with the luscious Norah. He tried the straightforward approach, but would come to the first hurdle, or rather *at* the first hurdle, and that was that; Norah would variously turn into some form of food, or a drink, or a box of tissues if Colin had eaten well that day.

Colin then tried something else. By concentrating on some neutral object while asking Norah to ravish him he hoped to sort the issue out. The only problem with this was that whatever he concentrated on seemed to override his sexual desires, and Norah inevitably responded by turning into that object before attempting to do her duty and ravish him.

Consequently he had been fondled by Brian Cann, the Von Trapp family, a wild (but gentle) boar, three dead faieries and a birthday cake made of plastic and wood which he had been given on his fifth birthday,

(this was to save his mother having to make one every year. She explained he could just pull out his own cake, annually, from under his bed. His Dad said it was even better than a proper cake because Colin would have it every day of the year, not just one day in three hundred and sixty-five, and Colin knew that, deep down, his parents only wanted what was best for him.)

Gradually, Colin came to accept the stunning Norah as just another in a long line of unattainable beauties, and even his hatred for Krap, who disappeared into the darkness with her each evening for a grunting, shouting session, seemed to ease slightly.

It was during her second evening with the two travelling heroes that Norah made a decision to tell them of her ulterior motive. Sitting around the campfire one night Colin was looking at the sky, watching the stars wink and shine and trying to keep his eyes off the gorgeous woman. He picked silently at his trousers to soften the hard patches between his legs.

Krap was poking the fire idly when he suddenly looked up, stared straight at Norah, and spoke in a low, menacing voice. 'I have tested thine enchantment and found it real enough, my beauty. But why art thou here? Why dost never speak now? Who art thou really?'

Colin was stunned by the melodious, lilting voice with which Norah spoke in response. He had lusted after her body, and now her voice gave him something else to fancy. It was as if she could drive men wild with her speech and that had been the reason for her silence. But now that she had to tell all she seemed relieved, as if a burden had been lifted, and the words poured forth in an endless stream of information.

'I am, as you rightly say, from the Syorks Tribe on a parallel world whose future is directly linked for inexplicable and ancient reasons to what happens on this planet.

'Our warrior arm is called the Beautiful Beaver Women, for is the entire planet populated by big-busted women such as myself who are desperate for the love and attention of a good man.' There then occurred a brief pause while Norah changed into a bag of crisps following Colin's natural climax at this thought. Once she was Norah again, she continued: 'Our head Beaver parted her lips to address our clutch (the collective noun for a gathering of Beavers).' She told us of the existence of this *Blue Peter Annual 1978* on the planet Threa and the machine which threatens the purity of the males who traditionally travel the cosmos from Threa to our world to mate with us. We were also told that this *Annual* was the cause of the Gods of the Animal Kingdom creating monstrosities which were upsetting the Balance of Nature on Threa by destroying the vegetation and this, for some mystical reason would also affect our planet.

Two of our warriors, Gash and Bush, were chosen to battle for the honour to travel through time and space to Threa, to help destroy this terrible machine. Only one warrior could undertake the task because the laws of physics, chemistry, biology, molecular relativity and domestic sciences stated that the hole wasn't big enough for both of the bare-chested, big bazooma'ed Beaver Warrior Women.'

Norah temporarily turned into a cold shower as Colin once more lost control as he thought of two beautiful Amazonian women trying to squeeze past each other to get into a small hole. Their sweat-stained breasts squashing together and rubbing against his face ...

'"On with the nipple-rings," shouted our Head Beaver, once more parting her lips,' continued Norah. 'The rest of the clutch watched in awe as lesser beautiful Beaver Warrior women attached the deadly devices to their mistresses' heaving, bouncing breasts. It was an incredible sight to behold.

'Gash and Bush faced each other in a circle of mud, for some reason that I am not quite sure of, and glared at each other with love and loathing, such being the way of beautiful Beaver Warriors. Ferocious would be their periods of anger and fierce would be their tempers yet all the time loving and loathing, loathing and loving.

'"Look at those two loving yet loathing Warrior women in that pool of mud," spake our leader, "let the contest begin."

'Our two Warriors hurled themselves at each other with such force that Gash covered herself in mud and caught Bush a glancing blow of great severity.'

At this point even Krap was fidgeting and trying inconspicuously to rearrange his loin cloth. It was only the fact that Colin had nothing left to spill that stopped Norah from turning into something else. Instead she just grew more and more beautiful as the floating melodies of her voice tickled the heroes' ears and caressed their inner thighs.

'Our clutch,' she continued, 'smiled at the terms of endearment that were hurled forth in the loathing and loving of battle before the heroic Bush was declared the winner. There wasn't a dry eye in the house.

'As Gash took her defeat gracefully and rubbed

soothing balms into her heaving mounds, Bush stood before our Leader and spread her arms out wide to accept the challenge. Unfortunately she accidentally hit me in the side of the face, I having encroached during the excitement of the fight, and I fell into the time and space continuum which happened to be passing by at that very moment. Gash will be so cross because she won't be able to come to Threa now I have filled the hole.'

'And filled it beautifully,' said Krap politely. Norah ignored him.

'A time warp or two later I landed in the courtyard of the faieries' castle. They quickly captured me, enchanted me, and you know the rest.'

She sobbed silently to herself with the memories of the foul and wicked things she had been forced to do in front of the faieries.

There they were then. Three people with the same quest. Norah and Krap wanted to destroy the BLUE PETER ADVENT CROWN, and Colin had to get to it first and recreate his beloved Susan before Krap smashed the machine. And all for the Balance of Nature on Threa.

Krap shifted over, put his arm round the sobbing Norah and tried to comfort her, while Colin admired the way her breasts retained their shape as they bounced up and down with her crying. He could see no evidence of nipple rings, but that didn't mean she had never worn them. Colin had to go for a walk to calm his thoughts and beat his trousers against a rock in a nearby river so that they would soften and dry before morning.

By the river Colin appraised his situation. On the bright side, there was the fact that, if he was to sire the

Niloc lineage of Galactic rulers sex was, presumably, somewhere on the horizon. On the dark side, he had to face the fact that, after sex, he would soon be dead. He thought of all the things he still wanted to do with his life, like become a rock star, or a world-class motorcycle racer, or go to bed with Michelle Pfeiffer ... (no ... he couldn't even contemplate that Michelle could be the mother of the Niloc dynasty. Could she? But how would he meet her? Where was she? Was she a shape-changer? Would she become a three-course meal when he tried to touch her? No, surely not. A faint glimmer of hope stirred his loins, but soon died.) He now felt that he just wouldn't have time to do any of them.

Colin desperately wanted to go home. He could ... he could hide. Yes, that's it. Hide. In the library. Or at home. He would be nice to Brian or become a recluse or something or anything as long as he LIVED!

He tried to explain all this to the Conqueror, but couldn't find the breath or the right words as he struggled day by day to keep up with the huge Krap's stride across the barren terrain towards the marshes and Snipe, the one-eyed monster. Norah would jog along beside the mighty man, her body tempting and full, making it difficult for Colin to run or even walk straight sometimes. She would still occasionally be tuned into Colin's thoughts, and many was the time she would turn into a large, pendulous breast with nipple rings and beaver's teeth. Then when she turned back to her normal incredible self she would have to run faster to catch up and that just got Colin all worked up again. The strange thing was that she never seemed to mind.

They would journey all day, Colin's trousers

crackling and softening finally as the sun rose high in the sky and he started to sweat profusely. They did come across a travelling band of Thargs once, but Colin was so preoccupied with self-pity that he hardly noticed Krap dispatch them with his mighty sword (even the killing frenzy seemed a little muted) and viciously stamp their instruments into the ground. Trumpets were wrecked and oboes were rent assunder. Krap did take a fancy to a rather natty trombone in bright pink which he hooked across one mighty shoulder as they continued their quest.

The danger or the quest weighed heavily on Colin's mind to the exclusion of all else – except occasionally that bronzed, bosomy body that travelled with them. But it was Susan he loved. Could he ever love Susan again, he used to wonder? Of course, the answer was always yes, if only because he knew that Susan would wait for him to come again in exactly the same shape as she started out.

In the distance strange and weird creatures, which were obviously products of the dastardly machine they sought, passed by. Most were too wary of the rippling pectorals accompanying Colin to bother them, but a vast herd of Unipedibrennansaurus did hop close-by at speed once, squealing their distinctive cries of 'Bug-Eraiye-Vee! Bug-Eraiye-Vee!' Krap swung and missed several times before felling one for food supplies, and there was a short break for a meal.

Colin sank deeper and deeper into despair, while Krap silently basted the meat until he discovered it was a self-basting Unipedibrennansaurus, at which point he left the joint to cover itself with juice and walked off to gather more wood for the fire. As he was hand-in-loin-cloth with Norah it was obvious that not a lot of wood would be found. It was a quiet, reflective time for Colin.

A herd of wildebeasts grazed nearby, apparently unperturbed by the three humans, Threans, or whatever they were. Two of the mighty animals came a little closer to crop the shorter grass, and turned to stare at Colin as he shifted uncomfortably.

Looking at those massive, shaggy heads with tiny little faces and small squitty eyes, Colin allowed his mind to wander temporarily away from the problems that faced him. I wonder what those beasts are thinking, he mused, as they look and graze over miles and miles of vegetation. They're probably thinking 'look at those adventurers. Lucky bastards! If only we could trade places with them and end our meagre existence of eating tundra, then crapping, then eating more tundra but this time with crap all over it and then crapping on the tundra with the original crap on it and eating tundra with two lots of crap on it and probably crap on it from another bloody wildebeast like that one with the haemorrhoid problem, you know the Grapes of Wrath and all that stuff, who continually lays cable about from his posterior and probably covers the stuff in wee as well. Why he can't use quilted bog roll, or why I can't use it for that matter and you three can I'll never know – or even a bidet – but then I suppose I wouldn't be able to wipe my enormous bottom with cloven hooves. And I suppose that a bidet in the hinterlands would be out of the question, being incredibly hard to plumb in, even though pressure joints these days have made welding and soldering obsolete and also those curly springs for bending copper pipes.

'Now, what was I going to do. Ah yes, shall I eat, or

crap? H'mmmm, decisions decisions. Never a dull moment being a bloody wildebeast.'

Colin shook his head and blinked several times. What had started off as an idle thought about the lot of wildebeasts in life had somehow become a complaint. It was as if the two beasts staring at him had transferred their thoughts to him. No, that couldn't happen. Could it?

And then came a great moment in History, which will go down in the annals of the Animal Gods' lives as one of the all time greats.

The Gods had decided to tune in to the tundra for a little bit of an update on how their vast herds of various beasts were wrecking vegetable life generally. They were just in time to hear one of the wildebeast say, 'Look at those wankers,' in fluent wildebeastean, which the Gods were of course familiar with, having partially invented the language before deciding it wasn't really for them because the grunting and snorting gave them sore throats and there were twenty-seven words for tundra, but only one for bidet and none at all for ballcock, and therefore giving it on to the first stupid thing to walk by.

'Yes,' replied the other great quadruped in the slightly gutteral dialect of Eastern Tundra Hinterland.

The Gods stared, gobsmacked at the scene they had witnessed, and knew that the moment would never be repeated. Oft would the moment be recited; the famous dialogue sketch between two great creatures of the pampers and, as with all such quotes, (such as 'Play it again Sam' and 'Beam me up Scotty', which were never actually spoken), the quote would be changed and manipulated to suit the occasion. Thus:

Wildebeast one. 'Look at those wankers.'
Wildebeast two. 'My bottom's sore.' Or,

Wildebeast one. 'Look at those wankers.'
Wildebeast two. 'Have you finished with the bidet?'
Or,

Wildebeast one. 'Look at those wankers.'
Wildebeast two. 'Be bop a loo la, she's my baby.'
(This one became perhaps the most famous of them all.) Or,

Wildebeast one. 'Can you pass the quilted loo roll please?'
Wildebeast two. 'Only if you've washed your hoofs.'
Or perhaps the all-time favourite in the Threan Old-Time Music-halls:

Wildebeast one. 'I say, I say, I say, this tundra is tastily crisp today. Though perhaps the particular acidity obviously derived from the urine could use a touch more alkaline in it. What say you mine fine four-legged friend?'
Wildebeast two. 'Aren't you supposed to say "Look at those wankers"?'

While they picked silently at their food, two heroes with dark and damning thoughts in their minds, and one enchanted shape-changer with very little in her mind but a large amount on her chest, a huge Brontosaurus with massive breasts hanging down from its stomach approached the area, scattering the herd of wildebeast far and wide. It sheepishly bent its long neck to look Colin straight in the eye. He was terrified and Norah turned into a quilted toilet roll.

'Hello.' The dinosaur spoke softly for such a massive beast. 'I'm Emily, and I may have a message for you. What's your name?'

Startled out of silent meditation, Colin started to say that he was not Niloc, didn't know Niloc, and wouldn't know who on Earth Niloc could be, but he might be able to pass a message on or else to Colin, though that wasn't him either, oh no, perish the thought, when Krap leaped up and sliced the dinosaur's head clean off. As the inane, inoffensive grin went bouncing off into the distance, the enormous neck spasmed, straightened, and crashed down onto Colin.

Black velvet curtains were drawn tight across his mind and a sense of loss and emptiness accompanied Colin to oblivion.

CHAPTER EIGHT

Discotheques were once fashionable among the tired and washed-up who enjoy touching consenting adults in places not usually touched by complete strangers without getting hit in the face.
From Sylvester's bestseller *The God Out There*.

While in the grip of the black stuff, Colin had the most incredible dream he had ever dreamed, and had he understood it, it would have changed his life once and for all. His scrotum felt as if a vampire had been incredibly thirsty and had drained his meat and two veg of all the blood that had previously lived there.

Only after about half an hour did several thrusting blood cells brave the elements and, being bored with the kidney area, come floating along the empty blood vessels towards the testes. They had arrived via both the left and the right ventricle and were obviously in a very dangerous mood.

'Hey blood!' yelled the red corpuscle,' I hear there's something gone down in the nut section.'

'Up rather, I'll think you will find,' said his friend. 'I do believe that that Krap ruffian kneed mine host in the goolies.'

'Yo, you've got to get up to get down, blood. Let's take a butchas.'

'I do wish,' admonished his friend, 'that you would speak properly and not in that fake cockney patois. It does not become you, it is not clever and it is definitely not funny. You always have to go too far, don't you? Why can't you just have a laugh and a joke like anyone else? But no, not you, you have to go one step further. Push it to its limits. God, you get on my nerves. Now just fuck off while I go see what's happening in the left leg.'

'Been there, seen it, done it,' gloated the red corpuscle, who didn't seem in the least put out by his friend's outburst.

And then – and here's the really interesting bit – the dream camera panned back and focused on Colin's inner-self, which was in a state of flux and confusion. His outer-self held him together, and in fact Colin had the very real impression that if it hadn't been for his outer-self, he would look a right mess and there would be blood and guts everywhere.

Jeez, he thought, he wouldn't be able to move or do anything, just lie there blob-like in appearance and just sort of rely on gravity and wind to affect his position. Or perhaps somebody would be able to carry him around in a bucket.

But here was the weird bit. How would he get upstairs, or eat, or go to the toilet? What about sex? And with what? How would he be able to get excited?

He could see it now. A rush of blood from one side of the puddle that was Colin to the other, while two savage beauties eyed him up in a most complimentary way. One would says to the other, 'Look at the size of his puddle. Jeepers Creepers, he's hung like a cow pat!'

Then, in his dream, he woke up to find that his reproductive organs had swollen in size considerably. No longer did he have a teeny tiny . . .

'Good grief,' escaped from his lips. His mother

burst into the room on hearing his cry, and his father followed closely behind.

'Look at that,' said his mother to his father in a 'told you so' sort of way. 'Do you see that?'

'It's not hard,' said his father in astonishment. 'What have you been up to young lad? You appear to have a rather swollen organ.'

'Well you wouldn't believe it,' said the young but big-balled and bulbous-membered Colin.

'Try me,' retorted his father.

'Well, I was trying to sit on my dick,' said Colin in a straightforward man-to-man sort of way.

'Mother,' spake his father, 'have you heard this? He says he was trying to sit on his ... WHAT?' He looked at Colin, who now started to realize that he was in quite considerable pain. His organ was a strange and foreboding colour and seemed to throb, and with each throb seemed to grow in size. There was a distinct correlation between the throb and the size. Colin was scared.

'Look Colin,' admonished his father in a father-to-son sort of way. 'How many times have I told you not to try to sit on your dick?'

'Well never, actually father,' said Colin truthfully.

'Well let's just put it this way then,' said his father gravely. 'This is the first and the last time I'm going to tell you. Don't sit on your dick, son; it hurts.'

With that, his parents rushed out of the room and slammed the door shut. All that was left to keep Colin company was his engorged penis and Krap the mighty Conqueror who stood like a brick outhouse at the side of Colin's bed.

When Colin finally crawled slowly out of the pit of nothingness he could smell a rich, roasting aroma from the fire. He part-remembered the dream, and had the sneaking suspicion that if he could think hard about the whole of it, then he would be able to make sense out of his life once and for all. And indeed, this was true. Had he taken time to analyse it the rest of his life as recounted herewith might have been quite different.

But he just looked up rather gingerly instead, quite forgetting the dream, and realized that they had moved on from where they had met Emily Brontosaurus and were now on the edge of the marshes. He must have missed the village of B completely.

The sun clung on to the sky, threatening to set but still blazing away. The second sun was just rising. This would be a long day, realized Colin. His eyes and head hurt, and his stomach rumbled to remind him that he had hardly eaten since embarking on the quest. Then he remembered the pizza, and saw Norah sexily licking her lips at him from the other side of the fire. To Colin's hunger and social frustration was now added embarrassment.

'So, Librarian!' ha-ha'ed the huge Conqueror, 'thou art once more in our land of living! Far have I carried thee and much have I slain in thine defence. We are,' he indicated the surrounds with one brawny arm, 'on the outer-reaches of the marshes. Eat now, for we still have far to travel.'

Colin took the offered hunk of roast meat and dropped it as it scalded his fingers. He gingerly picked it up again and blew on it, as much to dislodge the tiny insects that crawled all over it as to cool it down. Juggling the meat from burning hand to burning hand he wiped some grass off it and took a bite.

Quite unlike anything he had ever eaten on Threa, this meat was delicious and just melted in Colin's mouth. He wolfed the lot much to the amusement of Krap, who chewed a giant bone. Colin held out his hand eagerly.

'Can I have some more please?' he asked Krap. 'That was incredible! What is it?'

As the barbarian sliced another piece from the slab hung on a spit across the fire he thought for a while.

'I believe 'twas introduced to thee as an Emily Brontosaurus,' he finally said.

Colin's sense of loss returned and gripped his stomach. He retched violently. He couldn't eat a friend, or an almost friend anyway. The first thing to be nice to him on this journey and he was bloody eating it. Her. Bloody eating her!

Eating his friends, prospective or otherwise, reminded Colin of Susan, and he reached for the pocket where he carried his beloved. He touched the cold, comforting paperweight. He sighed with relief.

Krap guffawed at the jumble of scenes and emotions flashing through Colin's mind, then turned his attention to his pink trombone, which Norah had been idly fingering. He quizzically pulled it, so it stuck out straight in front of him, then tried to suck it. He finally tried blowing, and a low, mournful sound was emitted. Krap looked pleased with himself and continued to toy with his horn.

Suddenly, as if in response to the trombone, the longer grass on the edge of the marsh began to wave and rustle as if by magic. As Colin sat stock-still with a double helping of déjà-vu, Krap let go of his pink trombone and grabbed hold of his weapon. Norah was once again pushed to one side to hide in the long grass.

'Hide in the long grass until I have need of thee,' spake the man-mountain, before returning his attention to the motions before him. 'Aieeee, what sorcery is this?' he cried, and was about to strike when a tiny head on a long neck stuck up out of the grass.

Two sacks, or wattles, obscured its vision as they hung down over its eyes. A flick of its head and the sacks bounced back momentarily to reveal the scene to the creature and the creature's piercing brown eyes to the travellers.

'Hola!' it squeaked. 'I'm Percy, in the employ of Snipe. Who are you to summon my master so?'

The silence was broken only by the slaps as Percy continued to flick his head and the sacks plopped wetly back over his eyes. Then Krap bellowed.

' 'Tis I, Krap the Conqueror, come to speak to the one-eyed monster. Be about thine business, slave, and tell thine master I do demand his presence here.'

Two more identical heads appeared by Percy, and he flicked his head more vigorously now. 'Careful, barbarian. Don't get cocky. You might be able to fight and beat Thargs, but you couldn't lick me, pal. Not with my mates here for protection. This is Willy.' Percy nodded to the right and Willy flicked in response.

Colin was getting the hang of this. 'I suppose the other one is Dick, is he?' he asked quickly.

The three laughed hysterically in high, squeaky voices.

'Hear that?' cried Percy. 'Dick he says. Dick! What a plonker! Eh, John-Thomas. Fancy him thinking you

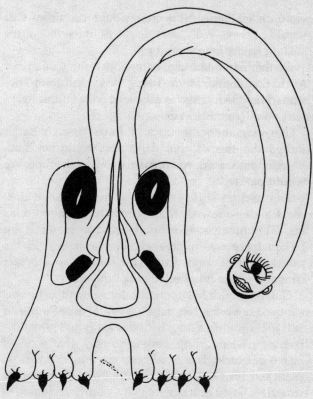

SNIPE, THE ONE-EYED SNAKE-MONSTER

Famed for its exploits in Threan coastal waters, this almost mythical beast bears a 'face' of agony, with 'eyes' of torment on its body. The 'eyes' are said to hold a man in a trance-like state while the neck uncoils and takes him from behind.

However, some spunky seamen who have taken their choppers to this specimen's head say that this is a load of balls. The beast, though, is known to stand its neck erect in moments of excitement, and to spit violently from its mouth when in a state of uncontrollable frenzy.

were called Dick. Now that would be funny that would. Percy, Willy and Dick! Sounds like three steam engines or something.'

Further extended giggles annoyed the Conqueror so that on the next flick, Percy, Willy and John-Thomas found the mighty broadsword only a pubic hair's curl away from their necks.

'Begone, annoying ones. I have thrown better things than thee off this planet and would not think twice about tossing you off also. Now fetch Snipe. We would parlay.'

The sentries stiffened, spat at the barbarian then quickly disappeared. Krap hardly had time to relax his taut muscles, and Colin had barely stood up before there was a great, boiling upheaval in the marsh waters, and Snipe the one-eyed monster dragged his mighty neck clear of the ooze.

Colin's mouth fell upen in astonishment as he was captivated by the two false 'eyes' on Snipe's putrid body. He couldn't drag his stare away to look at the thirty gink-long, three-gink-wide neck that writhed and straightened and arched gracefully down as would a snake, so that Snipe's single eye looked at the travellers – first at Krap, then at Colin. Somewhere in the long grass Norah Spleens turned into an economy pack of toilet roll.

'Who,' hissed Snipe, 'summons me with the Pink Trombone? Who?'

Krap raised his sword high, flexed his bronzed, sweat-stained muscles and screeched, 'I, Krap the Mighty Conqueror, oh vile and putrid beast. Thou wilt answer to me and mine Librarian friend or have thine head cleaved in two!'

Not a particularly smooth introduction, thought

Colin, but he was rather pleased at being called the Conqueror's friend.

The eye stared at Krap, unblinking.

'But,' hissed Snipe sarcastically, 'thou art no member of mine species. 'Thou art certainly not full-time member, and dost not act like polite, part-time country member, so why should I help thee?'

'I am the Conqueror, and thou shalt answer to me!' yelled Krap, as his sword hissed through the air. Snipe's neck curled with incredible speed and whiplashed out, caving-in Krap's ribs and breaking most of the bones in his body. The super-hero slumped to the ground.

'And thou?' asked Snipe quietly, eyeing Colin.

'Ah ... um, I'm a country member, sir,' bleated Colin, who was in complete shock.

'Ah yes, I remember. Librarian.' The word had an ominous taint to it as hissed by the one-eyed monster. 'What dost thou seek, Librarian?'

Colin was transfixed by the eye, but his peripheral vision embraced the lifeless body of Krap. It was some time before Colin could gulp the lump out of his throat and answer.

'Um we, uh, that is, I er – OH MY GOD! KRAP! Oh, dear God, no.' He broke the spell and rushed to the prone body of the Conqueror.

Suddenly he was alone. He had nobody to fight for him and no one to look after him, and he was on Threa and he couldn't get home and he was really, really miserable. He cried. And cried. Then he cried some more. He thought about Norah and the fact that he would have to look after her now, and he redoubled his crying.

In the first friendly gesture since his arrival, Snipe

gently coiled his length around Colin's neck and nudged him under the chin. Colin looked up, and through the tears saw a blurry, rather soft looking head with its single eye staring at him. For some reason he thought of his father and tried to stop crying, but even that memory was too painful and then his bottom started to hurt.

'Enough Librarian,' hissed Snipe gently, ' 'twas but a game that got out of hand. I know your quest, for I can read thine mind. Thou searchest the fabled Isla St Clair to destroy the evil machine that has been created for purposes other than planetary harmony. We ancient beasts of Threa have little truck with these new life-forms, and so needs must I help thee.'

Colin stopped blubbing at this show of friendship but still sobbed a little in posthumous regard for his friend Krap, who lay collecting flies and insects beside him. He was just about to ask this monster why he hadn't helped them when Krap was alive and then they'd have a better bloody chance of achieving their goal, when Snipe continued.

'Thou dost need the sword.' Snipe gently brushed Colin's cheeks with his lengths of cold, clammy neck. 'The one they call Pork.'

Colin gasped, as chapter three, volume one, page 976 of the *Chronicles of Ancient Threa* spread out before his mind's eye.

'Lo verily was there a fabled sword, one so powerful that it did drink men's souls and did seek vengeance and justice and should be used only in strict accordance with the instructions which are written in Japanese and are thus unintelligible as there are no Japanese on Threa. So verily does this sword Pork lead a life of its own.

'And yea was this the blackest of the black weapons cast from nigrate (NOTE: this is a substance very much like nigtare but stronger. And blacker. As Old Stig used to say "Give oi nigtare for buildings, but nigrate for mythical swords any day o' the week, m'darling.") 'Anyway, be'st thou careful should'st ever encounter it.'

'Take the sword,' soothed Snipe, and Colin suddenly realized that, high on the beast's neck, clung Norah. Even swaying about way up high she was sexy and composed, her breasts wobbling gently and her mouth softly kissing Snipe's neck. How she had got there he didn't know, but she was obviously going to stay there.

'Oh Snipe,' she was moaning, 'oh Snipe, you enormous hunk. Never have I seen such hunkiness. I must stay with you. I will serve your every wish. Oh Sylvesters! Come on baby let's get on with it.'

And Colin stared at her thunderstruck, as she went riding, riding, riding into the air aback the mighty Snipe. She didn't notice Colin and appeared to be in a state of sexual ecstasy; little moans and gasps escaped her perfect lips as they caressed Snipe's neck, again and again. She briefly turned into a box of tissues as Colin was transfixed by her pleasure, before she eventually broke all mental contact with Colin and turned her full attention onto Snipe. Colin felt alone and empty, as if someone next door had just moved away.

'The sword, 'tis the next clue on thine journey, for verily does not one single organism know of the whereabouts of the fabled Isla,' said Snipe with a huge grin on his face and a beautiful woman on his back. He flushed and breathed deeply. 'Take courage,

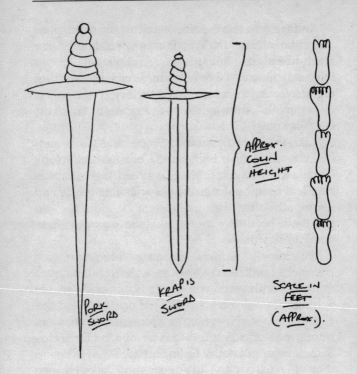

Pork Sword

Krap's Sword

Approx. Colin Height

Scale in Feet (Approx.).

WEAPONRY OF A BYGONE ERA

*As can be observed from the above scale drawing, Pork the
Soul Eating Sword dwarfed Krap's broadsword and Colin's
foot. Incredibly enough, the handle design of the two mighty
weapons is, on close inspection, remarkably similar, leading
to the oft postulated theory that they looked very much alike.
But just look at the blades, will you?*

oh brainy one, and sorry about your mate. And remember. 'Tis not what you do with it, but the size that counts.'

And Snipe and Norah disappeared. Just like that. Colin looked around and even the boggy surfaces of the marsh looked undisturbed. But standing next to him, seemingly balanced on its point, was a huge, shining, shimmering sword.

'The Pork Sword!' whispered Colin in wonderment as he almost forgot about Norah and the sounds of muffled passion that floated towards him through the mist.

'Yep,' replied the sword, though it was not obvious from where the sound came.

'You can talk!' cried Colin in amazement.

'Yep,' answered the sword.

'Um, well, how do you do. I'm Colin and I'm ...'

'I know,' interrupted Pork. He, or it, or even she, had a rather tinny voice, as if speaking into a car-phone through a tin can stood in a phone booth five metres away. That sort of voice.

'Well, uh, what do I do now?' asked Colin. He felt a little better now, with a companion, but hadn't a clue what he was supposed to do with it/him/her.

'Wait while I get my sowwwwwwl, man,' breathed the sword which leaped into the air and embedded itself in Krap's broken foot. Several toes fell off.

Colin looked away in disgust. 'But that's Krap!' he cried.

'Krap, crap, man,' replied the sword con-temptuously. It leapt off again. 'It's Krap with a silent K, man, and I don't dig no rap brother. I need me some sowwwwl. Ya dig?'

Colin recovered his composure a little, though his

underwear was definitely uncomfortable by now, and stood up straight. His trousers creaked slightly and flakes of 'stuff' drifted down his legs, both inside and outside the garment. He was shorter than Pork.

'C'mon, man, we's off to find Kew,' yupped the sword. It bounced lightly on the spot.

'Who's Q?' asked Colin.

'No man, not Q. Kew. He's the dude to get you into the Isla, baby. C'mon.' More bouncing on the spot.

Suddenly Colin remembered the quest, and impulsively snatched up one of Krap's toes from the floor. He stuffed the leathery, horny object into the pocket full of sick and amber. It was a wild thought, but maybe. Just maybe.

'Y'all ready?' asked Pork.

'What for?' asked Colin. He was still a little bemused by all this, but admitted to himself that he felt a bit better, even though the Conqueror lay conquered next to him. Maybe it was because the quandary of Norah had been sorted out for him and he could concentrate on the reconstitution of Susan.

'The jump, man. The jump. Let's go, baby.'

Colin was stumped. 'What jump? What do you mean?' He wasn't sure he could pick up the fearsome weapon, let alone jump with it. Oh, if only Krap were here. Well, he was here, but if only he were alive. A great sadness started to well up inside him.

'No, blood, not that sort of jump. Shia! Temporal time continuum jumping, man. We just moooooove our little selves over through space and time to wherever we's going. Capishe?'

The sword sounded impatient now, but Colin was still unsure.

'What, you mean like we get there now? Without walking?'

The sword stopped twiddling on its point.

'Yea, blue, the dude's got it! Like now, bro'.'

'But, but ...' Colin wasn't at all sure about any of this. He liked the idea of not walking, especially as the stiffening seams of his trousers were starting to chafe his thighs, but having seen what Pork had done to Krap, and knowing the sword's reputation for collecting souls, he was scared.

The sword laughed coldly. 'Ya'll afraid I's gonna take your soul boy?' it asked darkly.

'Well yes, sort of,' admitted Colin weakly.

'Hell boy, y'ain't got no rhythm, never mind soul!' and Colin involuntarily started to spin round on the spot, faster and faster until he could see his own face looking the other way. Then nothing. Black. Infinity.

Nothing disturbed the cold, clear air or the mountain goat which was urinating on a nearby boulder at the edge of the peak. The goat was called Frankie Forehead, but nobody knew that.

Nor will anybody ever know it. For that goat is now dead, having passed goat-water onto an electricity sub-station that was just behind the rock and a little way down the mountainside.

CHAPTER NINE

And now for a little bit of pixie magic.
From Sylvester's bestseller *The God Out There.*

The mood was dark and depressing in the hideout that was the refuge of the Yoof Twins, Gods of all Vegetation. Yoof, sitting on his haunches in one part of the shelter fertilizing a little corner of his domain, looked up at his brother.

'Oh brother mine,' he whined, 'What be'est thou preparing for luncheon? For am I hungered and in sore need of something to munch on.' (Yoof had decided to turn to poetry in his hour of greatest need, and it was getting on Untilatelyoof's nerves.)

'Mushroom bloody surprise,' snapped Untilatelyoof, who did stand by the fire stirring a bubbling pot. 'Mushrooms in a lemming-blood sauce.'

'What? But mushrooms are our creation, brother. What happened to Gnu stew or another? We should not eat our own stuff now. Surely we should slaughter a badger, or a cow?' said Yoof in his concerned voice. 'Lemming sorbet would be quite nice, with perhaps some flies, or the intestines of mice.'

'They are all run out, brother dearest,' said Untilatelyoof between gritted teeth. 'And yea, though mushrooms be of our creation, be these little bastards hybrids which have, of their own volition and free will, decided to spawn and grow and take succour from our other more important creations in the manner of parasites, or parachutes – I can never remember which.

'Thus have I boiled them so that they may not repeat their acts of heresy,' his voice became vehement and the strain of the last few months came to the surface. Spit flecked from the corners of his mouth. 'Yea verily shall we, by use of our digestive tracts, ensure that these little shites shall no longer our hard work bugger.'

'Calm down, calm down, Untilatelyoof. I totally agree, egad forsooth,' agreed Yoof, accepting the bowl of mushroom surprise from his twin. He stayed in his squatting position as he stirred the grey gloop with a rudely carved bone spoon. He laughed pensively.

'Knowst thou, brother mine, that these parasites be known as magic mushrooms by some Ungodly creatures? 'Tis because on our list of creations they never have featured.'

Untilatelyoof nodded his head, ground his teeth and started his repast. It was well known that mortal beings claimed that anything not directly created by the Gods was caused by magic, and that these items really did not belong in the scheme of things, lest heredity oust the Gods' abilities to be the only true procreators on the planet. And those bloody rhymes were getting right up his nose, big-time.

Having licked his bowl clean and then moved on to lick his brother's bowl clean, Yoof belched and created a pattern of fragrant daisies on the shelter wall.

As he looked, the wall started to swirl, and retire

and go out of focus. Yoof felt strange and lightheaded. He squinted at the wall, which rushed forward to greet him, and Yoof could see the daisies racing round and round, diving here and there, and hither and thither, and lo and behold, and suddenly Yoof sprouted wings without warning.

'I am off, brother dear. I can fly, I can fly! I shall now be gone and fly up to the sky!' cried Yoof (though Untilatelyoof only heard'Argh ya fack bazza bleugh wagh yablurry git,' though quite whose fault that was is anyone's guess) and Yoof leapt up and sped off for the clouds.

He soared way, way up high, all the while giggling and laughing and finding everything absolutely hilarious, and then he got a stitch and nearly crashed. He swooped and soared and glided (or glade) over the pampers plains of Threa. He stampeded the vast herds of wildebeast, and frightened the whores (collective noun) of Smelsingborgs and the tarts of Throbulets in the forest clearings with his high-pit-ched squeaky laugh.

'Oh no, I'm a goat!' giggled Yoof in prose as he flew on, on, onwards to the mighty mountain ranges on the horizon. And he passed over a Librarian or two, and the odd super-hero, but paused nary a while to speak or stop laughing raucously. He did not stop, nay, for his goal was the very peak of the greatest mountain of them all, Mount Ayne, whose craggy slopes stood lonely and proud and majestic before him.

And on his way did Yoof fly over a herd of pigeons, and did he crap on them to get his own back, all the while guffawing and screeching.

Yoof laughed at the breeze as he flew on and up

towards the snow-covered summit. He grinned when a swirling eddy of wind caught him halfway up, and chuckled as he was slammed into the nigrate slopes.

He chortled softly as he rolled over, face pummelled and bruised, to see his brother standing over him with concern in his face and the walls of their shelter very firmly about him.

'Groth! Did you see that? I flew! I flew! Did you?' strained Yoof in ecstasy tinged with the start of a big downer.

'No,' said Untilatelyoof sadly, and a little warily because that last sentence could have been prose or rhyme. 'It seemed to have no effect on me.'

'Ah well,' sighed Yoof as he gingerly got to his feet,' maybe next time we can have it in a cake, or even burn it and inhale.'

Untilatelyoof nodded, then spake softly. 'Did'st see our heroes on thine out-of-body flight brother dear?' he asked.

Yoof looked a little sheepish. 'Um, perhaps, but then again I'm not at all sure, twin beloved. Ah, I forgot to look, to tell you the truth. Sorry.'

Untilatelyoof frowned and turned his back on Yoof in disgust. 'And we have no more magic mushrooms,' he complained. Yoof shrugged stupidly, and went to another corner of the shelter which looked as if it needed fertilizing.

CHAPTER TEN

Se itl ucif fidgnid aerevahuoyod?
Uo yerof ebeg apehtn opu xim dn ae lgn imts ujsdro wod?
Pleh na cewd na yenom fos to lsu dnes.
Advertising literature from the DNA, National Dyslexic
Association, as it would appear to Brian Cann, Clacton Librarian.

t was Susan! Susan with a bright yellow halo around her gloriously naked body. She knelt over Colin and gently slapped his face with her breasts. Great, pendulous breasts, swinging this way, then that way, then opposite ways, then figure of eights, then looping the loop.

'Niloc,' she hissed. 'Niloc, let's do it. Come. Let's get this dynasty on the road. Oh take me, take my virginity. Take it all. Oh God, you're the best ever. Ever. None of the others could ... ooooh yes! Yes I mean it. Oh darling, fill me up. Yeah baby, ooh, give it to me. Unh Unh Unh.'

As Colin looked down his body he saw John-Thomas pop up from between Susan's parted thighs. Flick of the head.

'Oh bloody hell!' croaked the slave. 'There's a horrible musty smell down here. Sort of fishy too. Yuch!'

Colin tried to shout 'shut up' but it came out as 'your turn Brian'. Hallucination. Dream, thought Colin bitterly.

'You might be hallucinating but I'm not, har har, snort,' grinned Brian, as he crashed his spidery body repeatedly against Susan's buttocks. On hands and knees she turned her head and smiled raggedly at Colin.

'You've had your chance,' she gasped, 'now I can take my true love. Oh Nairb! Nairb!' She pursed her lips and ooooohed.

Colin thought he'd burst. In fact he did, and the assembled throng were roaring with laughter when he opened his eyes.

'Ho ho ho' boomed a large, fat man dressed in a red robe trimmed with white fur, who was stood before Colin, next to Pork.

'Yo, blood, those were *some* pictures there in your brain, man. You're diseased!' screeched Pork giggling.

Colin slowly got up and pieced together what had happened. The 'jump' had obviously knocked him out en route to this place, which resembled a clearing in a jungle, with lianas, or lanas or lamas or whatever they were hanging down from the huge trees, and dense undergrowth all around.

Pork, the Father-Christmas-type figure, and six goblins stood before him, all still shaking with mirth. Colin did a couple of inconspicuous knee-bends to reduce his protrusion and quivered as the slimy, cold feeling spread down his groin. His temper suddenly snapped.

'You – you utter bastards!' he murmured.

'Sorry?' asked Kew politely.

Yes! That's it! The realization was stunning to Colin. Kew! This bloke was Kew and no wonder he hadn't remembered him. The references in the Chronicles were in code. Of course!

'And lo, shall one who finds the black soul-eating

sword of Pork be warned; should that person not know the rightful owner or rightful master then verily be there just one thing that can help him and that is to say to that person "fuck you".'

Except that it wasn't 'fuck you', Colin realized, but 'for Kew'! It was obviously a typographical error. Oh praise be! Wait till readers of the Chronicles heard about this. What new horizons it would open up for them. It made a whole lot of sense of one of the paragraphs that had baffled Threan specialists for ages. Maybe he'd be more acceptable to Threan scholars now and even make some friends! Wait till he got home!

'For Kew,' he said out loud, savouring the new meaning.

'Fuck you an' all boy,' boomed Kew angrily. 'Get thee down, shep,' he exclaimed. Then his mood softened. 'You come far?'

'Oh yes, uh yes, far,' stumbled Colin.

'Far what, peasant?' yelled Kew autocratically.

'Um, far sir?' pleaded Colin who was now getting very worried at this character's manner and volatility.

'What's my name, by all that's purvis?' screeched Kew who was going red in the face now.

'Kew, sir,' mumbled Colin.

'So? You come far?' repeated Kew threateningly slowly.

'Um, far Kew, sir.'

'You Throbulet's gusset!' screamed Kew. 'You cheeky bastard of an infertile Smocwoo!' He loomed large over Colin. 'This is my sword. Do you know who it's for?'

'Er, for Kew, sir?' guessed Colin not very intelligently and very quietly.

'You barbarian's armpit!' yelled Kew. 'You cheeky, rotten Throbulet dropping! Now bugger off before I do you in. Go on, bugger off!'

The jungle clearing shimmered, waved and was replaced by a jungle clearing exactly the same, but with a silver jeep instead of his tormentors in front of Colin. Or maybe the clearing was the same but the tormentors had gone, thought Colin. The lamas were still there, hanging from the trees and ...

'Enter me,' cooed a soft female voice. He heard it echo clearly around the clearing.

'Susan?' he cried, twirling around and seeing nobody.

'No, idiot, the jeep,' said the jeep, impatiently.

'Oh, I see,' said Colin. He didn't move.

'Get in,' said the jeep even more impatiently.

Colin approached rather warily and opened the door. Sliding into the driver's seat he saw no steering wheel, but a dashboard full of little knobs and buttons and different coloured lights. The door slammed shut after him and he jumped.

'Welcome, Earthman,' said the jeep in that rather pleasant, sexy female voice. 'English language mode engaged. Are you ready for a blow job?'

'What?' asked Colin, rather taken aback and pushing backwards into his seat away from the speaker from whence came the voice, but not too hard and not too hastily.

'Sorry, vocabulary correction,' corrected the jeep. 'Are you ready to go?'

'Go where?' asked Colin, who felt a little deflated now.

'Why, to the Isla St Clair,' said the jeep in a surprised tone. 'Why else would you be here?'

'Oh, well yes, I suppose I am,' said Colin, 'but I don't know how to drive.'

'Leave that to me, and just listen to the guide tape. We have Keith Richards or Lorraine Kelly. Please advise me regarding your parents.'

Colin looked a little surprised, but felt a little warm glow that someone was bothered about him and his life. So he sat back in the seat and stared into space as he spoke. The jeep moved smoothly forward and started to gain speed.

'Well, there's my Dad. Oh, Dad's OK really, what with my Mum working every night, you know. I think she works at GCHQ or the Foreign Office or something that's Top Secret because she never tells me where she's been and her make-up's always smudged when she gets in, and she's always really tired so it must be a very strenuous job. All my uncles say she's a really good pro' (that's short for Professional you know).

'They're not really my uncles at all but Mum says I've to call them uncle; I suppose they're secret agents, you know, like the *Man From UNCLE*, and they used to buy me presents when I was younger or send me to the pictures when they had something Top Secret to discuss with Mum at home. That was when Dad was at work.

'Well, anyway, Dad's OK but I think he got a bit clumsy after he lost his job. It was probably why he lost it to be honest, but I feel really sorry for him the way he just seems to have cups slip out of his hands and fly across the room every day while he washes up. Hah! They very nearly hit me, you know, but I know he can't help it.

'And when he dropped that electric fire in my bath,

well! He was mortified! I mean, it's totally under-standable and I think he was very relieved when he realized it wasn't plugged in and that was why he shouted and swore at himself, to sort of tell himself off and let the tension escape. Poor man.

'And when he accidentally spilled that gallon of petrol over me well, it's a good job he couldn't get that lighter to work when he tried to start a cigarette. Tension again, I suppose, poor old soul. Funny, he doesn't usually smoke but I suppose this self-guilt thing got to him after the accident.

'Come to think of it, we didn't even have a car, so Lord only knows what he was doing with that petrol. Ah, I feel really sorry for him. It must be the pressure of not working, I suppose.

'It's terrible really, to hear him shout and swear like that so often, but I try to soothe him by telling him not to blame himself and saying that he should cheer up, it may never happen. And then he makes that little joke about it was nothing to do with him and it already happened twenty-two years ago (though last year it was twenty-one years and before that twenty, so I know it's what we call a running joke or gag because it's always being updated), and then I think he feels better, and the washing-up seems to be such good therapy for him. I love the old chap really, and I know he loves me. Just can't bring himself to say it, but that's all right. Some men are like that. I read it somewhere.

'It's weird really,' chuckled Colin almost to himself, 'you think your situation or life is unique, but really it's pretty normal and there's loads and loads of people out there just like you. Imagine that.'

'I'd rather not,' replied the jeep sleepily. 'Error

correction in English language mode. Please advise me regarding your preference, not parents.'

'Oh, sorry,' said Colin, who felt as if a huge load had been removed from his shoulders and simply slung over his back. 'Preference for what?'

'Keith Richards or Lorraine Kelly?' reiterated the jeep.

Colin had never heard of either, so he said 'Keith Richards, please.' The commentary tape clicked itself into place as if by magic.

'Thnah thruh muh munh wanh thuck unh,' droned the tape.

'I think it's broken,' said Colin.

'No, it's perfectly OK according to my sensors. I have heard this one before, you know,' said the jeep testily.

'Unth manh muh wunh thitweath man hunth wanh,' continued the tape.

Colin tried to ignore the sound and paid closer attention to the scenery. Jungle had given way to forest, and the jeep ripped through a strange line of waving foliage some three metres wide and a few inches deep. Strange, thought Colin. Still, it takes all sorts.

Suddenly the tape cut out.

'Intruder alert. Back seat. Intruder alert. Back seat,' breathed the console, so sexily that Colin was part way to an erection before he understood the message.

'What?' he gasped, sitting forward and hitting his head on the dashboard as the jeep screeched to a halt. He never did hear the answer.

CHAPTER ELEVEN

'When my baby comes,
Dee dum dee dum,
Ooh la la la la laaaaah,
Crepe Suzette Whoopla!'
The first verse of the Lithuanian Eurovision Song Contest entry for
the year 2019, which will come tenth.

He came round in a large, damp, musty grey room with just one door which looked securely bolted and barred. A table and two chairs were in the middle. He was slumped in one chair, and as he raised his aching head he saw in the other … a Tharg!

Colin gulped in shock and his brain fed pain and despair throughout his body. A Tharg had captured him! He looked quickly round the room, as two pairs of piercingly red eyes followed his gaze in silence. No way out, he realized. He looked up towards the huge slabs of nigrate that formed the roof. Or at any rate used to form the roof, for they were no longer there. In fact there was no sign of them, just a thatched cover. How did he know that huge slabs of nigrate had formed the roof, he wondered. His head hurt and he was scared.

'Hello, hello, hello,' mind-spoke the right-hand head of the Tharg. 'Now then, young fella m'lad, tell us who you are and things'll go a lot easier for you. Who are you and why were you in the celestial yet secret customer tour jeep with restricted access for the Isla St Clair? H'm?'

'Bastard,' chipped in the left-hand head straight into Colin's mind.

Colin was a little taken aback, but started to gabble. 'Well, I'm er Colin, Colin Saw and I, ah, live in Clacton and work in the library and I came here with Krap who's dead now and we met Snipe and...'

'Liar!' yelled the left head mentally as Colin's fingers felt the reassuring contours of the paperweight and the toe in his pocket. 'Dirty stinking liar! Let me have him Sarge, I'll get the truth out of him.'

'Now, now, Corporal,' soothed the right head in calming thought-waves. 'You see, ah, Colin, was it? Yes, Colin, if I let him have you then he'll just rip you apart. That's the trouble when one gets promoted beyond one's twin, so to speak. So it's much easier to just tell me the truth and we'll get this little misunderstanding cleared up. Now, tell me the truth, please?' he prompted.

'But I am,' wailed Colin, 'I am, I am, I am! I'm Colin Saw and I really do work in the library at...'

'You scum!' screeched the left head viciously and pictorially, 'you lying, toadying Throbulet's groin of a snivelling git! You're here to interrupt the Tharg sexual organ fast-breeder programme, aren't you?'

'Back off!' shouted the right head non-verbally.

'Back off be buggered,' thought the left head, 'I'll make him talk. I'll have him, you'll see! Tell me, you're here to cut off our balls again aren't you? You're trying to destroy our vaginal introduction programme too, aren't you?'

'No!' commanded the right head with a picture of a large stop sign, his stare never leaving Colin's face. Colin could feel the twinge of an early mind-lock, and tried to clear his thoughts.

'Now come on, Colin,' said the right head softly and internally as the Tharg gently patted Colin's hand, 'the truth now, or I won't be able to restrain him. Now, who's Maria and where are these hills that sing? Tell me or else he might take over the body regardless of the fact that I'm his superior, and where will that leave you, eh?'

'Spattered over the walls, that's where,' growled the left head. 'Just like all those embryonic sexual organs would be if you had your way, eh? That's right isn't it?'

Colin was really frightened now. None of this registered in his brain and he was about to open his mouth and admit to everything including the Great Train Robbery when the cellwall exploded. Bricks, mortar, thatch and déjà vu fell on Colin from all sides, and dust filled what was left of the room.

'Bastard!' sneered the left head as it parted company with its neck.

'Now maybe we can sort this thing out,' wheedled the right head as it, too, popped off to expose a neck pumping blood, and fell to the floor with the blade that had severed it.

' 'Ello, 'ello, 'ello,' echoed eerily around the debris as blood (green) mingled with dust (grey) and Colin choked and tried to wipe the slime (brown) from his face (white with a hint of grey).

As Colin mechanically started to wipe his glasses to see what had happened he was grabbed by the left shoulder and bundled towards a huge hole in the wall. He briefly caught a glimpse of the glistening, bronzed cellulite which swept him outside into the harsh daylight. Then he had a proper look at his saviour and his mind was shocked at the recognition.

Chapter 10, volume two, Page 1037, *Chronicles of Ancient Threa*.

'And lo! For 'twas Ken Clarke!

'He of the rippling fat and the moon-shaped face.

'He of the belly bellow.

'He of the loud voice and the obnoxious attitude.

'He of the small dirty privates and the private dirty smalls.

'Yes he of the single trouser-leg and the chequered history, of the unspeakable apron and the unthinkable taste. "Ken, Ken, Ken!" crowds would shout. "Temptation, thine name be Ken Clarke!" '

Colin was not at all sure what Ken Clarke had done or achieved on Threa, but this be certainly he all right. The large, porky figure breathed heavily as it struggled to calm its quivering flesh. Clad only in a one-legged pair of shorts, Ken Clarke wobbled before Colin and gasped.

'Librarian?' He bent over, hands on his knees trying desperately to catch his breath. His breasts splayed out over his belly, which in turn settled over his thighs. 'Thatcher!' he shouted, invoking the long-forgotten name of a Threan arch-criminal and Demi-God. 'I could do with something to eat after that.'

'Yes, yes,' said Colin in answer to the question. 'I'm the Librarian, and I'm here to destroy the machine and recreate my friends.' He pulled the paperweight and the toe from his pocket and held them out in explanation. Cold vomit dripped off the items. Ken Clarke grabbed the toe and bit a chunk off before Colin could stop him. He spat it out and gave the stump back to Colin.

'Pah! The sauce is all right but the meat is tough, too tough. If this is all you have you can keep it. Sylvesters! These tourists!' Colin felt relieved to get the artifact back following the misunderstanding, albeit somewhat smaller than before.

'What are you doing here anyway?' he quizzed Ken. But as Ken wheezed something about balances it all leapt into Colin's mind with blinding clarity.

Chapter 10, volume two, page 1037, footnote in small italics nearly impossible to read, *The Chronicles of Ancient Threa*.

'And Lo! shalt he who be known as Ken Clarke be once, and once only, heroic in the restoration of the Balance, though that Balance be sorely out of whack and be truly large and cumbersome to accommodate one of such girth.'

Balance, thought Colin. The Balance of Nature! Of course!

Ken nodded his agreement, obviously reading Colin's mind.

'So you can take me to the Isla St Clair?' asked Colin tremulously, his thoughts now of Susan, and only Susan. Oh, and Krap. Oh yes, and destroying the machine and all that, but mostly of Susan. And just a little of Norah. But not too much. She was becoming a memory. Just a dream from his past.

Ken wheezed and his body rippled in response. He pointed to the ground. 'Here,' he coughed, 'you're here.'

Colin looked around in amazement. He saw nothing but thick foliage and the blown-up prison cell, but it all suddenly took on a different feel. There was almost an aura about the place, pulsating and vibrating with life, and new hope.

So this was the place, the shrine where Krap and Susan would be reborn. Where Colin would play God and be his friends' creator. Their futures lay in his pocket. If only he'd brought a piece of Norah with him he suddenly thought. He could have remade her without the enchantment – but then he decided that it was best to stop thinking about this particular 'what-if scenario', as Brian used to say.

Colin was joyous, and followed quickly as Ken beckoned him forth and led him down a narrow track. Their way led through the very heart of a seemingly endless jungle. The crude path had been hacked through the dense undergrowth some time ago and the lamas and lianas hanging from the tree canopy above their heads dangled ever closer to the intrepid pair. The air was moist, humid, and even seemed to steam a little. Colin started to sweat almost as heavily as Ken Clarke did when he was at rest. There was a constant noise above and all around them; the chittering of chits and the chattering of parrots, mynah birds and other exotic animals only briefly glimpsed.

Ken struggled, and sweated, then struggled some more. He stopped frequently and looked as worn out and unhealthy as Colin's great-uncle Hubert had just after he died. Colin got increasingly frustrated at the slow pace during what he saw as the final part of his quest. So close, and yet it'll take all blooming week to get there, he thought.

So when Nature called on Colin by ever so slightly pressurizing his bladder, he thought he might as well stop and do it properly, as opposed to in his trousers as previously. He could easily catch up with Ken Clarke in no time at all. After all, a little privacy was called for in this most intimate of moments. Ken leaned his bulk against a huge tree trunk and Colin took his chance.

'I'm going for a wee,' he told the fat man, indicating the jungle to his left. 'I'll catch you up.'

Ken coughed and hacked. He spat out a huge gob of phlegm which was sort of grey coloured and which slowly dribbled down his chin and blobbed to the floor. 'A wee what?'

Colin was puzzled at first. 'Oh no,' he cried gaily a few seconds after, 'no, you know, a pee.'

'A wee pee?' asked Ken as the paroxysms of his latest wheezy fit subsided.

'You're too fat mate, hello give us a nut,' chittered a particularly bright green parrot above them.

'You know, relieve myself,' said Colin in exasperation.

'Be dead by sixty, you mark my words, who's a pretty boy then,' retorted a jet-black mynah bird above the jungle screech.

'What of?' continued Ken.

'Being fat, of course, pieces of eight, pieces of eight,' said the parrot descending to a lower branch.

'My wee,' whined Colin. 'Oh look, go on, get going and I'll catch you up in a few minutes.'

As Ken struggled off he whipped out a pudgy arm with a speed that didn't even give the fat time to wobble, and grabbed the mynah bird by the neck. He tore it from the branch it had settled on to be closer to the pair of travellers and which it had considered a good vantage point for more gratuitous insult hurling, and bit its head off. He mumbled something like 'dead by sixty eh? Well sod you,' and spat out the beak, throwing the rest of the carcass at the parrot, which squawked raucously and flew off straight into a nearby tree. It fell, stunned, to the floor, revealing itself to be an incredibly intricate bio-genetic model of a bird, created by some fiendish monster and controlled by a model aircraft handset. But nobody noticed.

Colin wandered into the jungle to look for a good place to wee and was not particularly surprised to see a brand new urinal hiding behind a tree. He casually wondered how it came to be there as he used it, then turned to look around as he struggled with the rusty zipper on his trousers.

Nothing but trees and foliage, and narrow shafts of light filtering down to highlight the giant praying mantises that stalked the jungle floor looking for carrion. Colin started feeling a little uncomfortable on his own, and turned to go. But where the urinal had been there was now a sparklingly new washbasin complete with his favourite soap, and a roller towel for drying his hands on. Not for one second stopping to consider the implications of this piece of enchantment, Colin ran some water and revelled in the softness of the soap on the skin of his hands. He rubbed the bubbles up his arms, and laughingly rubbed some all over his face. He looked slyly around and, seeing nobody near him, he carefully unzipped his trousers once more and took the opportunity to clean his willy, which had started to feel a little cheesy.

Dabbing himself clean on the towel (so much better than those warm air things, as he always said to anyone who would listen) he felt a whole lot better and quite refreshed. Now to find the path and catch up with Ken Clarke again.

'Over there, past that small bush,' pointed Krap.

'Great, thanks,' said Colin and set off jauntily, thinking now only of getting back to the path to find this machine and recreate his friends. Krap, the mighty warrior, would thank him and probably make him a blood brother or something like that.

'Beware impure thoughts, oh spotty one, lest ye be disappointed when thine head be hewn from thine shoulders,' muttered Krap as he followed Colin onto the path.

Colin was embarrassed. 'Oh, um sorry, no well, maybe just pen pals or something,' he stammered.

And Susan.

Oh Susan.

Colin daydreamed of his love, his one and only. Cor, now *she'd* be pleased that he'd brought her back to life. Maybe she'd even snog him or . . .

'Huh!' grunted Susan beside him. 'More likely my fist in your mouth than my tongue, you little git. I'm saving myself for a REAL man.'

Colin was not surprised by her reaction but even so . . . woah!

'Woah!' he cried. 'Susan?' He turned to face . . . Susan!

'But how?' he questioned, automatically touching the paperweight that still nestled in his crispy trouser pocket. 'How did you? And Krap?' he started. He looked around, but there was nobody there except Krap. Krap! Where was Susan? Colin held his head and his vision became a little shaky and blurred. A tremendous pressure was building up inside him and he almost fainted. He fell to his knees and then something struck him. To his surprise it was a thought, as opposed to the usual blunt object.

'Norah?' he whispered. 'Norah is that you?'

And the vision of loveliness that was Norah Spleens in the buff, totally naked, with not a stitch of clothing to be seen, took shape and stood before him.

Her breasts seemed to rest on the top rim of his glasses and as he was on his knees, his eyes were right in line with her gorgeous ... oh what's it called, he wondered dreamily.

Colin briefly stared at himself then Norah shimmered back into view.

'Yes, oh Librarian, 'tis me.'

Then Colin remembered, and a horrible sinking feeling came to his stomach and rented it indefinitely with a three-month break clause.

'What, and *you* were Krap?' he started slowly. She nodded. 'And Susan?' She nodded again and her bosoms rippled smoothly, nipples joggling on the spot. 'And ... the urinal appeared and disappeared, then the sink, confirming Colin's feelings of horror. What he'd done in that sink, and in that urinal, and all along it had been Norah!

'Oh Norah, I'm so sorry. I wouldn't have done it if I'd known it was you,' he whined, with a pathetic little yelp at the end of the sentence.

' 'Tis of no import, Librarian. I was sent by Snipe, my new master, to guide you in your travels and on your quest and to forewarn you of dangers that lie ahead, but I see thou hast Ken Clarke for to do that for thee.

'Thus was my appearance unnecessary, and did I hide behind a tree. But you did come across me, or rather piss all over me and at such proximity was I captured once more by thine mind patterns.

'Be careful with thine thoughts, Colin, until Snipe does reclaim me, which he will soon do for have I sent word. I am not yet completely healed of the enchantment and will still take the shape of thine greatest desire, as you see.' She slid her hands alluringly down her hips, accentuating the curves and pressing her bosoms together with her upper arms.

As Colin shuddered and felt the familiar groinal warming, Norah turned into a couple of turkey burgers with chips.

Colin got up slowly and started to snivel. His greatest, greatest, absolutely most important desire and he could never do anything about it. Except wee on her and wipe his willy on her unknowingly. He blew his nose on Norah then unhappily trudged off after Ken Clarke. His despair and misery was complete. He couldn't cope. He was sticky and hot and messy and spotty and OH GOD IT WAS HORRIBLE. He was miserable, dejected, depressed.

He never even looked back as Norah turned into Colin, drank a whole bottle of Benylin, two bottles of Calpol, swallowed a bottle of paracetamol, lit a joint and ten Embassy Regals, stood in front of a speeding bus and stabbed, hanged and shot herself while slashing her wrists and masturbating wildly until finally she was swallowed up by the earth.

Colin slumped his way forward.

'Blimey,' wheezed Ken, as Colin rounded the next bend. 'Cheer up for Sylvester's sake or I'll probably top mes'en too.'

Colin ignored him and padded past the fat, sweating mass that clung to another tree whilst gasping and panting for air.

'Wait, wait,' puffed Ken loudly, 'for doth there lurk danger or some peril ahead.' This time Colin took notice and managed to lever his depression out of the way and replace it with self-preservation. He looked ahead and saw that the path widened slightly before turning another corner. He noticed then that the cacophany of the jungle had ceased, or at least didn't exist in this neck of the woods. Or jungle. It was quiet. Deathly quiet except for irregular asthmatic wheezes as Ken fought for his breath.

Colin hardly dared go on, for something told him he was at the end of the trail. He rather stupidly shut his eyes and stepped slowly round the corner. Having shut his eyes Colin didn't really want to open them again in case there was something scary there. He managed to scrunch them up then peer carefully out of a tiny slit in one that he barely managed to make. His mouth dropped open as did his eyes at the sight before him.

The path they had been following opened out into an enormous clearing just ahead. Light streamed down almost joyously onto lush green grass, which had been carefully cropped to an even length. But it was a green that Colin had never seen before. Dark and sort of full and, well, really green. Angels sang and orchestral string sections played joyously in his mind as Colin beheld, in the very centre of the clearing, a table. And on that table was the machine.

No.

THE MACHINE.

The boxes and tinsel and sticky-backed plastic that held his dreams were there, in glorious living Technicolor. The only way for him to redeem himself and regain any measure of self-respect stood before him, bathed in golden sunlight and beautiful, just beautiful. And there was not a soul in sight.

A large moth flew into Colin's open mouth and he snapped out of the spell that had bound him. He tried to spit the thing out but only succeeded in swallowing it whole. At the thought of the insect wiggling about inside him he was violently sick, and splattered the jungle floor. The moth shook its wings clean of vomit, tasted some with its long tongue, and flew off.

Ken pushed Colin forward and whispered, 'Get on with it. I'll look out for trouble.' He weebled off to the far side of the clearing and sat down.

Walking slowly forward, Colin almost stopped breathing, such was his awe. He held out his arms, as if blind. Nothing stirred; the whole world had ground to a halt and everything in it awaited this moment of truth. He crept closer and closer, his mind a whirl of whirly things and images of Krap and Susan and tinsel.

Then he reached it. He put his hands out and touched the screen, ever so gently. A tingle coursed through his body from finger tips to toes as he touched, caressed and fondled the contraption. Colin hadn't a clue how to start, so he threw the toe into the tube where he had seen those old people throwing things. The screen coughed and lit up, an eerie green glow in the gathering gloom, for the sun was starting to set. Row upon row of letters appeared on the screen. Colin panicked. This was obviously Krap's genetic make-up; he knew that DNA looked something like this from that film he'd seen with his Mum. But he didn't know what to do with it, if anything. So he hit the keyboard with his eyes scrunched tight closed, and waited.

With a flash of light there appeared before Colin a small, dwarf-like being with a badly made pink loin cloth, which contrasted starkly with his green-hued leathery skin.

'You're not Krap!' screamed Colin in a panic. Ken heard him and started to amble over.

117

'No,' coughed the dwarf. 'I'm all the opposites of Krap thanks to you mucking about with my DNA. My name's Park, I'm a Jew and I'm just a little sick. You know, whereas Krap was Krap, non-conformist and healthy. And big,' he added looking up at Colin.

'Thatcher! Sick Park,' swore Ken. 'What do you think you're trying to do?'

'Do?' yelled Colin, panicking even more now and turning to the dwarf to take it out on him. 'Do? You're supposed to be Krap, not a sick Park!'

'Whatever I am you created me from Krap's DNA,' accused Park as he stabbed a crooked finger at Colin in a poorly sort of way.

'You fool,' muttered Ken with a jeer, 'a sick Park is all you come up with? Be about your task Librarian, and destroy this machine. I can endure a sick Park if it means that this loathsome contraption is no more to meddle with the Balance of Nature.'

'But I want Krap back,' bleated Colin. 'I mean, you know, the way he was.'

'Then stuff Park back into the machine and reverse your instructions,' hissed Ken, oblivious to the protestations of the dwarf. 'But be quick about it.'

'But I couldn't,' wailed Colin. 'You're asking me to injure a sick Park. I couldn't.'

Ken lifted the dwarf with a grunt and stuffed him head first into the tube which seemed miraculously to expand to take the bulk like a snake swallowing a small rodent. The screen flashed on and Colin blindly hit the keys. Another flash, and there stood Krap. Huge and magnificent as before with loin cloth and broadsword.

'Krap!' swallowed Colin in stunned yet proud disbelief. His delight was shattered however by a

```
TRIDZ TGZTS ZBZBW ZZ FFO WO LBCAS SOKSZ BZRZH
ZOIZW OZOUZ UZAAZ ZA TIP SZ OZRHZ ZNZZR HESUS
ZCRAB ZSCST ZLNZB NZ ZUX ZI ZSIZB OLFOZ CZGHE
KKTXE SKZTS LKTON SZ SZE LZ ERELB BOWZT ZEIRS
EINEE RGOZS EZGYX ES EXS EX TZZJZ ZNZUZ FTEHZ

VZZRZ ZCZCR ABSXE SX ZTX ZL ZZOZZ HZMZA OCAZC
IZBON KXEST IHSZC RE EPZ IZ ZCITA UDATN TFZOZ
NMUCS ZNHNO ITERC ES EZF UC KZTTD UZSEI TZPII
ZXXES ZAOZT ZGOMI TC HTZ ZE EOTOE ZMSOZ ZUTIT
SEXZM GELFZ HTITI TZ EZZ YZ NERER EEBZZ LZZCZ

TSXZN ZXESO ULZCO KR OPB ZY RKRZL LANDU DNOZL
IZEAZ ZEZNM EZLRZ ZT BON KZ SAZLF SSZOO ZPZEZ
FZSEX ESNZH ZEABO RT TIE ZW SZYZH OREGG UBSZF
FTEYZ ZHZIZ STZPU GT TAZ OA ZBYAN GRGXL ZBZUZ
YZXZP OZGZE EZOMG OE VZR CZ ANGZP SINAZ IZCZZ

XESER HHZXZ EOPAM SE RDO ZS NNZET EZTIA ZKZZZ
SEXES CIZNI FTYZM NR ZOZ TA AZNUZ XESNC OZZZZ
ZZAAL EZLZZ ZXIEY ZU TRA FS ZIRZH OOPZF AZZSZ
ZZPUS ZXZIZ EZLHZ TO ORZ TZ EDZZO ZZZFN ITERC
ZEBAS TARDS ZLZHS ID DIY IN GXZZT ANIGA VXESZ
```

DNA: THE BLUEPRINT OF LIFE

*This is the screen display that Colin saw on inserting
Krap's toe into the Gods' machine. Hence it shows what
Krap is made of.*

*By looking carefully at the code we can deduce that, for
example, Krap's parents were not married at his conception,
that this conception was overtly sexual in its nature, and
that it probably took place in a Welsh holiday resort.
However, most of the 'description that is Krap' remains
hidden to all but the most dedicated decoders.*

mental disturbance that suddenly came to their minds.

'Some sod's messing with the BLUE PETER ADVENT CROWN!' said one.

'Sylvesters! Let's get them,' cried another.

'I'll turn them into a Throbulet's scrotum!' shouted a third. The others laughed.

'You're obsessed with sexual parts you are and it isn't healthy in a God of your age,' said another with a giggle.

Confused images of Thargs and old people and other monsters too hideous to describe floated in front of Colin's cerebral eye.

'Quick,' shouted Ken, 'destroy it! We are undone.'

'No, wait,' panicked Colin, frantically reaching for the paperweight and throwing it into the tube. As Ken moved closer to the machine Colin willed the screen to come on and started to hit the keyboard maniacally. The machine gurgled, and a flash of light produced ...

'Susan!' cried Colin.

'Ah sort of,' answered the bespectacled face. There was something familiar about it, though the body was most definitely female in all the right places. But that chin!

'I'm Cozzie, a cross between Colin (that was your puke, remember) and Susan, or Susie. Lush eh? Oh, and you're quite a cutie. What d'you think?'

The creation was pouting at Colin and started smoothing its hands over its voluptuous curves as it posed. Meanwhile Ken belly-flopped onto the table, crushing the machine into a thousand flat bits.

Colin didn't know what to say. He was rent asunder by the predicament. Could he love that body?

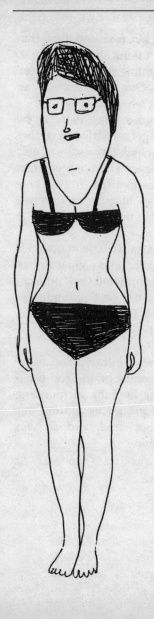

COZZIE

The slightly bouffant hairstyle only adds character to the femininity already oozing from this rare beauty. Colin added the bikini due to his own modesty, and also because he couldn't exactly remember what those bits looked like. Cozzie's voluptuous curves were everything Colin ever dreamed of, and he drew this picture soon after his adventure so that he could keep it in his wallet. He also keeps several stick-on faces which he feels represent the realistic outcomes of cosmetic surgery had he managed to return with Cozzie.

Yes. Could he love it with his face and that chin sticking out of it? He couldn't think straight.

'Come on,' coughed Ken, getting shakily to his feet. 'They'll be here any minute. Our job is done. Krap and I will hold them off. You two escape.'

'Ooh not me, lovey,' boomed Krap gaily as he picked at his nails. 'I'm off to get some decent clothes and a damned good bath. Just look at the state of me.'

Cozzie grabbed Colin by the arms and dragged him off to the opposite end of the clearing, from where there came the commotion of hideous, malformed bodies crashing through the undergrowth. Colin struggled to get to his feet.

'Hang on,' he complained, as Cozzie rounded a corner and smashed Colin's head into a gigantic tree trunk. Bit by bit Colin's mind shuttered itself off from reality, and the confusion of the past few minutes turned into a sublime inkiness that preceded unconsciousness by about a second.

A passport control booth with infrared and ultraviolet scanners and an obnoxious, brain-dead occupant winked briefly from the foothills surrounding the Isla St Clair. Teasingly promising a duty-free shopping experience it disappeared, and all was peace and tranquility once more.

CHAPTER TWELVE

'It's all going to be fine once we're rid of the rodent Portillo.'
From Ken Clark's bestseller *Chaos Theory*.

Untilatelyoof and Yoof stood at the entrance to their hideaway. Their despair and despondency at the non-appearance of the mighty Krap and that other person was so deep and all-pervading that some of the grass at their feet had actually turned yellow, as if it had been growing under a plank for the last three months. They swiftly apologized to it and boosted it with a quick creation spell. It returned gladly to its former verdant lushness.

They had even reverted to their original names of Yoof and Untilatelyoof, as opposed to Untilatelyoof and Yoof, though nobody had been aware of the change in the first place so it hardly mattered.

They knew that they fought an increasingly desperate battle for the survival of such species as their Poisonous Vixenboots, and the small, yellow Feeyournostrils, but could not find any solution that did not require the arrival of the Conqueror to smash the machine for them. With no new giant animals created from the past there just might be a chance for them to redress the Balance.

'Maybe I could help you,' came a voice from the corner of the shelter. The Yoof twins jumped;

although the voice was mellow and soft, they had not been expecting guests.

'Who be there?' barked Yoof. He looked, but could see nobody.

'Sorry?' came the voice.

So, it wasn't a dog, thought Yoof cunningly. That was a relief. An invisible dog was all they needed now.

'Who art thou? Where art thou?' asked Untilatelyoof in Desperation, the international cross-cultural multi-specied language developed, it was said, by Sylvester to communicate with all his creations. It was this language most often used in mind communications on Threa.

'I am Blair, the chameleon. I am here in your shelter, in the corner farthest from you.'

'But we can'st thou not espy,' complained Yoof, looking at his brother and getting a blank stare in return.

'Look, I told you, I'm a chameleon. What the bloody Thatcher do you think chameleons do? You know, what are they really, really good at?' snapped the invisible Blair.

There was a long, excrutiating silence from the Gods. They knew of Shamoleon, which was a type of grass that grew in clumps so small that only a single stem was involved. They also knew of Camels, which ate Shamoleon by the clump-full and little else, but apart from that no, they had no idea.

'We bloody hide!' said Blair in an exasperated voice. 'That's why you can't see me. We hide and we are very, very bloody good at it.'

'Ah!' said the twins together, their faces still a mask of non-understanding.

'Good,' said Yoof uncertainly,' that be very good, oh chameleon. But move a little, so that we mayhap spy thee out.'

Time ticked by slowly, but nothing happened. The Yoofs stared fiercely into the corner until their eyes hurt. Nothing.

'Want me to move again?' asked the chameleon from behind them.

'Sylvester, um I mean He Who Shall Remain Nameless! What treachery is this?' shouted Untilate-lyoof, his illness forgotten as he whirled round and took up the long forgotten 'how to deal with just about anything with your bare hands' defence stance.

'No trickery,' said Blair smugly from the corner of the room from whence he had originally spoken. The Gods whirled back to face it/him/her. 'I said we were bloody good at it didn't I? Hiding, you know. We take the colour, texture, whatever of the thing we stand next to or in front of and bingo! Can't see us! Now, I can help you, as I said.'

'But thou art of the animal,' he spat, 'kingdom,' spoke Yoof. 'Why shouldst thou wish us to help?'

'There was a pause, and a deep, invisible sigh, though still no sign of any movement. 'I don't want you to help, I want to help you.' Another sigh. 'Nobody can see us, right? We can't help it, we just blend in, and very good we are too. So nobody remembers us, nobody helps us and the Gods who created us abandon us and just don't bother with us anymore. So we had a meeting, and figured that if we chuck in our lot with the Gods of Vegetation in this unholy war against the Balance of Nature then we could really improve our status and even maybe ...' the speech trailed off into silence.

'Maybe what, oh helpful one?' enquired Yoof gently.

'Well, maybe get an everlasting supply of Blue-fannie grass, which is our staple diet and a great aphrodisiac and only mildly hallucinogenic and is currently being stamped out by all those bloody wildebeast out there that the Animal Gods created.' The words came out in a great rush of emotion and the sorrow and the anguish was plain for all to hear. Yoof looked into the corner. Great concern showed on his face and a warm, fuzzy emittance from his persona enveloped the area.

'Of course,' he said, as he twaggled his fingers and a pile of succulent Bluefannie grass appeared and just as rapidly disappeared as the invisible (or rather extraordinarily well-camouflaged) chameleon ate it with much slurping and noisy chewing and belching but no apparent movement.

Yoof and Untilatelyoof conferred quietly and mentally in one corner, then returned to stare at the apparently empty spaces at the far end of the shelter.

'Yes, oh hidden one,' began Untilatelyoof, 'thou can'st help in our fight to balance Nature and its creations. Thou must go forth, stay hidden and contact one Krap who be a mighty barabarian and also a smaller one who doth travel with him. Bring them here with great haste for can they destroy the BLUE PETER ADVENT CROWN, I know it.

'Then, when the Bestial Gods can no longer create such base and vile monsters from old bones and soil can we, mine twin and I, get started on getting the Balance of Nature on this planet back into Balance.' He sighed. 'Ah, but that we were able as you to camouflage our divine selves and then could we

Threan woodcarving entitled
'CHAMELEON PARTY AT THE OLD GRASSY
KNOLL'
(reproduced here by kind permission(ish) of the Notcalc
Library).
According to ancient legend this was a favourite party place
for chameleons; indeed the keen-eyed observer may see
seventeen different family groups enjoying themselves in
the above print which was discovered (and accidentally
pocketed) by Colin whilst working in the 'Mythicalle ande
Magicalle Beasties' section.
Chameleons being generally rude, aggressive and secretive
creatures, it is not entirely clear why this particular spot
was favoured, nor why the shop (seen left) needed to be so
close by. When asked in a rare interview, 'Whatte doth do
withe ye fupofitory?', Wankbreak (Lord High Chief Master
of the Ancient and Magical Order of Chameleon; seen above
grooving near the boulders) is recorded only as saying, 'Go
fhove it up thine arfe'.

destroy the machine without help. But alas and alack we cannot and forsooth would we be found out and very likely exterminated.

'Now go little one, and return with our heroes.'

The twins were really quite excited. Here was an ally who could go anywhere unnoticed and who would surely be able to find their one remaining hope and thus end this uneven struggle. In fact, in their excitement they failed to realize that they had said find 'Krap the mighty barabarian' instead of barbarian. A barabarian was a large mushroom-shaped tree-climbing sloth-type creature of Ancient Threa. Blair was wondering where he was going to find one of them, especially one called Krap with a small mate. Still, that Bluefannie grass tasted awfully good.

Yoof moved over to the entrance to pull aside the lama curtain that disguised their abode so that the chameleon could start its quest.

'Careful,' warned Blair, 'I'm over ...'

A soft squelch and a spurt of red blood told Yoof that he had accidentally stepped on the chameleon which, even near death, blended in with the floor so well that all the twins could see were the red entrails splashed across the floor.

'Clumsy bastard,' whispered Blair as he died.

'Oops,' breathed Yoof, looking down gently and with disappointment at the insides of the corpse.

'Best find another I suppose,' chipped in Untilatelyoof, sombrely.

'How? I can't see them. That's why I stepped on it,' said Yoof, who was by now angry and depressed.

They both sighed heavily and their black moods returned. There would be time to bury the poor creature later. Or eat it. Now was a time to reflect.

CHAPTER THIRTEEN

'There is light at the end of the Chunnel.'
From Ken Clarke's bestseller *Chaos Theory*.

C olin woke up and got out of bed. As he walked over to the bathroom, expecting any minute to hear his father yelling in his ear, he fell into a deep ditch and suddenly remembered where he was.

He scrambled his way out of the ditch, which was twice as deep as he was tall. In the twenty minutes or so that it took him to climb the soft, sandy walls, he gradually pieced together what had happened to him recently, though his head hurt and felt like a pickled egg.

He had succeeded in his mission. The BLUE PETER ADVENT CROWN had been crushed beyond repair and it was unlikely that the shower of old people he had seen before would ever be able to mess up an advent crown to the same dangerous extent. He had returned Krap to his original state, though something still did not seem right. That comment Krap had made when asked to fight was totally out of character. Still.

And Susan! He had actually recreated Susan. But if only that vomit had not been on the amber when he'd done it. His heart was stabbed by a pang of hopelessness. Susan with his face? Then he thought about cosmetic surgery. Yes, that was the answer. They could go back to Earth together and he'd work extra-long hours and she could have her face remoulded and then with that body and her eternal gratitude, well! He got so excited that he almost failed to see the drawbacks to his plan which were twofold.

Firstly, where was Susan? And secondly, how would they get back to Earth?

Dark despondency threatened to cut off the day-light as Colin plumbed the depths of despair. He looked around the countryside for any signs of Susan as he nervously brushed the sand and grit from his trousers and jacket. Nothing but rolling meadows, hedges, trees and a dragon. No sign of Susan. He had never really thought about getting back from Threa to Earth.

Sure, he'd wished he'd been back a few times, but all his hopes had really been pinned on Krap, either in original form or recreated, and now Colin was alone he had not a clue what to do.

'Susan!' he yelled. 'Oh Susan, Susan, where are you my love?' He degenerated into a sobbing heap. Then he stopped.

He looked up. A dragon?

But it was gone.

No it wasn't, it was right behind him!

He whirled around and fell over. Looking up, the beast's massive snout was only inches away from his face. He scrabbled to get away, being only too aware of the roar of flame which would surely at any moment fry him to a crisp.

'What isssss it, little thing?' boomed the dragon in an almost American accent. A waft of stale, putrid, carnivorous breath, with a heavy hint of garlic,

THE DRAGON
An old Smegma spell-song that was very nearly discovered
by Colin in the library at Notcalc goes like this:
>*Dragonne dragonne burninge brite*
>*Flying through the wintere nite*
>*Always looking for a fite*
>*Only stoppes to have a rest*

Well, now we know that they cannot spurt fire, can't fly and
are generally quite cowardly. However, the timbre of the
whole spell-song leads us to believe that the point to notice
is that dragons do use toilets and wipe their bottoms
afterwards. Or maybe lick them clean, it's hard to say.
That's folklore for you.

engulfed Colin and he would have been sick if he had had anything to bring up. It was a horrible reminder of those Throbulets and Colin prayed with all his might that someone would behead this thing as well, and quickly.

'No, don't burn me, please, don't burn me, I'm all alone and I don't want to be burned,' he sobbed.

'Pah!' spat the dragon and green snot flopped onto Colin's lap. 'We don't burn, we have no fire. How the Hell would the Ice Dragonsssss, those popular, almost mythical, beastsss ever ssssurvive with a damned flame-thrower insssside of them? I admit my breath ain't what it ussssed to be but that ain't no reason to ssssay I can burn things. Pah!'

Colin felt a little reassured. As he stood up to let the dragon snot dribble to the floor he looked warily at the huge, scaly monster and its incredibly sharp claws.

'Well what do you want then?' asked Colin sheepishly. He then decided that sheep were probably a staple diet for this beast, so he straightened to try and assert himself. He failed.

'Ah, but it'sssss what do *you* want?' responded the dragon with an air of superiority. 'For I am Lord, massssster and creator of all you ssssssee.'

Colin was confused. 'But I thought that, you know, there were Gods and DNA and natural selection and breeding programmes and things to create stuff. I didn't know dragons did it.'

'Pah,' spat the dragon and Colin neatly side stepped the phlegm. The beast's head came a little closer, the breath a little stronger. It continued. 'Godsssss? Schmodsssss. There are no Godsssss. I'm the only God around here and if I want to create thingssss then I bloody well will. I jussssst don't feel like it at the moment.'

'Brilliant!' said Colin, who was infused with new hope. If this was true then maybe this dragon could get him back to Earth, or help him find his friends, or create new ones for him or something. 'In that case ...' he started and got no further.

From the clear blue sky there came a mighty bolt of lightning, which struck the dragon and fried it to a blackened crisp in seconds. A deep celestial rumble echoed around the countryside and sounded very much to Colin like 'Bollocks'.

All was still again except for the smoke rising from the carcass. Chunks of flesh peeled themselves off (obviously a self-carving dragon, thought Colin wryly) and Colin found them actually OK, if a little chewy.

With his belly full of medium-rare chargrilled dragon he took stock and decided to walk to the village that had just appeared on the far horizon. It looked pretty small but at least he might find someone with some kind of idea as to how to get him and Susan home. If he could find her.

What did she call herself now? Cozzie? No, she'd always be Susan to him, regardless of her face. It was what was inside her that counted and made her so special. With renewed vigour he set off across the fields of rippling grass.

By the time he reached the village Colin looked as if he had been dragged through a hedge backwards whereas he had, in fact, walked through three hedges forwards. Thankfully, the few inhabitants he saw looked largely human, and human peasants at that, seemingly untroubled by Thargs or monsters or beasts or Gods or anything as they went about their daily tasks. And they all seemed to know him.

'Hey, Niloc. Where have you been?'

'Looking a bit rough today Niloc. Been flanging your schlobber have you?'

'Niloc! What's the lucky creature this time?'

'Woah, Niloc! Give me some skin babe. Smart dudes! Old Nnac's been after you and he's roaring, man.'

All these references to Niloc made Colin nervous, and he shuddered at the reminder that Terminal Four was still out there somewhere trying to kill him. But in reality all that seemed part of a distant memory, and he reckoned it was probably best to keep quiet and just grin inanely, so he did. As for what a schlobber was and how one flanged it he had no idea.

Finding Nnac seemed like a good idea, seeing as Nnac was supposed to be looking for him, and it was made easier by the large, hand-painted sign over the biggest wattle-and-daub building in the village, which read:

'YE NOTCALC LIBRARIE AND YE SEAT OF ALL REFERENCE AND LEARNING. PROPRIETOR MR NNAC.'

Something struck Colin as familiar but the connection escaped him on the soft breeze that blew through the village of Notcalc. As he entered the building a short, grey-haired, wizened old man shuffled up to him.

'Ah, Niloc. Been flanging have we? Oh that I was a hundred years younger. But me, I'm Nnackered, har har snort. Get it?'

Again, familiarity beckoned but took a left turn just before it reached Colin. He nodded dumbly.

'Well, well, no time for that now. Please be so good as to trot along to "Ye Badde and Cruelle Ancientte, Evil Deedes and Othere Naturalle Disasters of Assorted Varieties" section and sort out the scrolls into some kind of order. Had rather a run on them this decade and we mustn't confuse the customers, har snort.'

And so Colin found himself working in the Notcalc Library, much as he had been in Clacton. After three days of this he came to certain conclusions regarding this situation, and had served no customers at all.

Notcalc was a small village of no more than thirty people. Mostly they turned the sod and tilled the soil, but all this was primarily to feed, as well as themselves, Nnac, who was known as the Keeper of the Scrolls. He looked after the library, which housed, incredibly enough, the accumulated learnings of the planet over the eons of its existence. There were scrolls and parchments dating back to the time of the Smegma, an early race in the development of the humanoid species on Threa. These were kept on shelves similar to those in the Clacton library, and categorized in sections by age and author.

Nnac had been Librarian and Keeper of the Scrolls for some four hundred years, and was ageing and wizening now to the extent that he had to train a successor. He had taken on as apprentice one Niloc, a local lad who looked, apparently, remarkably like Colin, but who had a way with women in the immediate areas – and with any other animal worth getting to know.

It was not unusual for Niloc, good apprentice that he seemed to be, to disappear for days on end with the latest love of his life, only to return at his leisure and continue to work until his next conquest. Nnac was quietly amenable to this because, as Colin found out, Niloc's filing was exemplary and there were not exactly a lot of people or other things visiting the library nowadays.

Presumably then, Niloc was away at the moment and Colin did nothing to suggest he was anyone but the wayward apprentice, though he suspected they were different enough for anyone in the know to notice. However, everybody seemed quite content to accept this new, quiet, efficient Niloc, and Colin's only worry was what to do if Niloc ever turned up. He did hope to have a plan by then, but it was very hard to formulate anything with any expectation of success.

Meantime, Colin almost gave up all hope of finding Susan, or Cozzie. Discreet enquiries in the area were met with blank stares or nudges and winks in a most distasteful and suggestive way.

He determined that, much as he had written himself back to Earth the last time with the help of Wealthy Vicars, he should do the same this time as it was all he could think of. And so, in the long hours between closing and opening time, Colin started to commit to paper the events of the last ... however many days, even weeks, it had been ... in the hope that he would return to Earth on completion of what would be volume five of the *Chonicles*.

It was very difficult trying to remember everything in the right order and then write it down with enough Lo's and Verilies by the light of a spluttering fat lamp onto parchment with a quill. Niloc apparently slept and lived at the library in what was called 'Ye Ofice', so while Colin's labour was difficult, it went unnoticed and unquestioned.

One night Colin decided to take a break at around midnight; though he couldn't be sure that it was around midnight it just felt like midnight. (His watch had stopped so he never wore it, and consequently had not brought it to Threa where he wouldn't have been able to keep up with the time phases anyway.) He needed to get some air, away from the acrid smoke of the candles and the swirling words of his writings, so he thought to take a stroll through the village.

Everything was quiet and a full moon or two cast an eerie yellow glow over the rude dwellings. Colin started to shiver, even though he wore his jacket and the night air was not all that cold, and he was on the point of deciding that maybe it wasn't such a good idea to be out at this time after all, when he caught a glimpse of something moving in the small graveyard at the end of the main village street.

Torn between absolute fright at the types of horrors that awaited him and the certainty that whatever it was he would now probably have to write about the bloody thing for the sake of eventual accuracy and therefore a return ticket to Earth, Colin stood rooted firmly, stiffly to the spot. A few seconds later, which felt like hours, he felt the hairs on the back of his neck stiffen. He became convinced that some sixth sense was warning him that there was something ghastly behind him. He turned around quickly, eyes tightly shut, and slowly opened them bit by bit.

Nothing.

He whirled around to face the graveyard once more and caught his breath as he saw an old, stooped figure shuffling towards him dragging a ... a ... a man-sized sack behind him with some difficulty.

'Nnac!' cried Colin, the relief in recognition of this far from supernatural object overwhelming.

'Ssshh!' hissed Nnac, caught unawares and guiltily letting go of the sack, which fell to the floor with a dull, lifeless thump.

'What are you doing?' asked Colin in a loud whisper.

Nnac approached him. He was covered in dirt and grime, and looked troubled.

'Look,' he said quietly to Colin, looking shiftily around in case anyone was listening. 'I may as well tell you Niloc. I found this scroll, see, in the store-dungeon of the Library and, well, I'm not getting any younger, and you know I thought that it might be fun, so I studied it and now,' – the words came out like a torrent now; Nnac seemed relieved to be able to tell someone – 'I am a Necromancer. Have been for a few weeks, actually. Oh, I'm not particularly proud of it but you would have found out sooner or later so I may as well tell you myself.'

Colin was stunned, but something stirred in his mind that demanded clarification first.

'You mean you can raise dead spirits?' he asked agog.

Nnac looked confused. 'Dunno, but it raises mine,' he retorted in a stage whisper.

Colin persisted, the idea swirling around before him like a beanfeast in the first stages of having cornflour added to it.

'You can talk to dead bodies and return their spirits to the land of the living and actually ask them things and they have to tell you because you brought them back and it works with any dead thing?' he garbled.

Nnac had a look of realization on his face now. 'Oh,

so *that* is what it means. No, I must mean necrophiliac, then. I'm always getting mixed up between them. Must be the 'romancing' bit of necromancing makes me think of my schlobber.'

Colin felt sick as his hope evaporated. 'You mean that you . . .' It went unsaid but Nnac nodded, grinned and shuffled off to his house with the sack in tow.

'Only bit of pleasure an old man gets now,' he murmured. 'They don't tell and nor will you, young Niloc, not if you wants to keep your apprenticeship.'

Colin wandered back to the library in a daze. He heard the disgusting sounds that started coming from Nnac's hut, all the groaning and schlomping and stuff. Colin shivered, locked the door and spent a troubled night in Ye Ofice.

Then it happened.

On the fourth day, Colin was just getting out of his sleeping furs in the office when he heard, through the closed door, a mumble of conversation in the Library. Knowing it to be too early for opening time, he silently opened the door a crack and gasped as he witnessed the scene.

There was Niloc, or rather the person he assumed to be Niloc. He had returned! He looked exactly like Colin, except for the absence of spots and a short, luxurious moustache which looked very trendy indeed. He wore a loin cloth only and was heavily muscled. And he had a sort of . . . a sort of glow of confidence about him that Colin had only ever seen on toothpaste advertisements. Nnac was talking.

'Out last night, Niloc?'

Niloc looked at Nnac strangely. 'You stupid old git, of course I was out. I told you I'd be away for a week with the "Major Is Now God on Earth" society.'

COLIN   NILOC

Colin's memory and descriptive comparison of Niloc to
himself using two passport photographs and some Tipp-Ex.
Note the general all-round sturdiness of Niloc's body, the
bull-neck and the trendy hairstyle. As for the moustache,
well, it's not hard to see why Niloc was such a favourite
with the ladies.
Colin would later use this picture, which he drew on Earth,
as a target for his high protein/weight-training regime.

'Oh yes,' nodded Nnac absently, 'that fantasy group of yours.' He sighed. 'I've told you that MINGE is no good for you. There's no such place as Earth and there's no super-hero called Major and it's unhealthy in a lad of your age.' He cocked his head in interest. 'Get any flanging done?' he asked with a cackle.

'Woay! I should say so,' gloated Niloc. 'There was some bint there called Cozzie. Woah, the body on that! Bit on the ugly side, huge chin, but who looks at the mantelpiece, eh? We flanged all night, and the things she did to my schlobber! Well! Kept getting my name wrong; calling me Colin, but other than that she was all right.' Hands on hips, he thrust his pelvis forward several times and grunted delightedly.

Cozzie! Susan! Colin pulled on his trousers and jacket in a hurry and rushed out of the office.

'Where?' he cried at the two astonished faces. 'Where is she?'

Niloc recovered first at the unexpected apparition, which somehow imparted a 'this could be you if you're not careful son,' type of feeling to him, and he grabbed Colin by the throat.

'Get lost, creep,' he growled, 'she's mine.'

With an almighty shove he pushed Colin across the reception area. Colin marvelled at the smoothness of that muscle action as he crashed heavily into the Crime and Catastrophe section (so re-named by Colin because he felt that 'Ye Badde and Cruelle Ancientte, Evil Deedes and Othere Naturalle Disasters of Assorted Varieties' was too complex a title, and the new one reminded him a little of home), just as a British Airways Executive Lounge crashed heavily onto the Notcalc Library, flattening it completely with a satisfied tannoyed departure announcement.

'Well, well,' said Brian. 'Young Colin eh? Where have you been then? You're late and we have customers waiting.' He took the ripped piece of cardboard from Colin's hand. 'British Airways to Florida eh? We must pay you too much, har har snort, eh? Well, that's fine for a weekend away but please do not dress for work the way you would for your holiday. You know the rules, grumpf har har snort.'

Colin looked down at himself. Trousers, shirt, jacket, no socks, shoes or tie. He picked himself up from the foot of the Crime and Catastrophe section.

Bugger you, you're talking to an inter-galactic hero and I've just saved Threa.

'Um, I'm sorry Brian, I don't know what came over me,' and he sloped off to the office to find his slippers. They'd do until lunchtime.

He was back, true, but he had been so close to bringing Susan back with him. So bloody close. He cried in the office, out of frustration and emptiness, then went out to face the Throbulets. He knew better than to say anything to anyone. He had some thinking to do first.

CHAPTER FOURTEEN

'I still can't hear you.'
From Sylvester's bestseller *The God Out There*.

News of the crushing of the dreaded machine took some time to reach the Yoof twins, as the jungle was so dense on the Isla St Clair that every tree had to tell every bush, and every bush had to tell every lama, and every lama had to tell every fungus and so on and so forth until the news finally reached the edge of the jungle. Then it rushed across the open plains to the Yoofs.

Of course, as in all verbal messages that have to travel vast distances with only the help of vegetables, something was lost along the way. 'The machine has been destroyed. Hurrah for the vegetation!' had become 'What d'ya mean big boy? How far is the ventilation?' The Yoofs sent word back through a particularly long grapevine that what they had received was obviously important but garbled, and it was three weeks before the original message came back in an intelligible form.

After some celebration in their home, the twins ventured forth. They followed their roses and eventually came to the clearing in the jungle, where the Bestial Gods still bemoaned the loss of their machine. They had been trying to piece it together again, but had succeeded only in creating a handy piece of furniture for your doll's house and something rather useful for Mothers' Day. The Yoofs stood at one end of the clearing and announced their arrival with loud, aggravating laughter.

'So, brothers of ours in name only, hast thine plan been thwarted. Hah!' spake Untilatelyoof. 'Where ist thy sting now, eh? Thou art not so bloody cocky now, beasts of the forest!'

Roger, the Cat God, lost his temper immediately, and created from his own ribcage a huge, mad lion which charged at the Yoofs. But they just laughed and politely asked a tree to fall on the animal, crushing it some six metres from them.

'Ho, 'tis more than we can stand!' cajoled Yoof insolently. 'Hast thou nothing bigger than that? Oh, but that machine ist broken. Shall we help them repair it, brother dear?'

The Yoofs set off across the clearing. Untilatelyoof deliberately ground the cuban heels of his snake-skin cowboy boots into the remains of the keyboard. All Hell broke loose.

The Bestial Gods started hurling various life forms at the Yoofs, but as often as not ended up flinging them at each other, and thus tended to choose small, soft, furry creatures as far as possible. The Yoofs grew weeds and lamas around the place so that the clearing was quickly filled in. The noise of Gods screeching and shouting at each other carried a long, long way.

'What?' roared a voice above the din, and the spontaneous creation and scrapping stopped. Everyone looked round, then gulped and looked up. The clouds rushed about the red sky and finally created a huge face, bleary-eyed and with about four days' growth on it.

'What is going on?' spake again the voice, this time from the heavenly face above the Earth.

'They started it,' said Yoof rather lamely.

'Ooh, my bloody head!' complained the celestial face, ignoring the Threan Gods as if they didn't exist. 'What time is it? What are you doing waking people up at this time of the wossit.'

As nobody had invented the watch yet, not being sure whether it was a vegetable or an animal, Untilatelyoof plucked a dandelion clock and blew the seeds into the air. The face sneezed. He blew three times before clearing it completely. 'Six o clock,' he said calmly.

The face roared. 'Bugger, I said I'd be at the taverna at seven, and I haven't even had a shave or a shower yet. Now you lot stay there and I'll get back to you in a little while. Then I'll sort out this mess once and for all. And shut that noise would you?'

The voice disappeared, as did the face.

The Gods looked at each other in awed silence, and then fell to the ground to pray, rather loudly, to He who shall remain nameless. Yoof couldn't help making a few daisy chains appear, and Untilatelyoof flicked a few sly begonias here and there. OK, they'd settle down and wait for Sylvester to come back, but they could have fun anyway.

Sylvester forgot to get back to them, due to large amounts of nectar and honeyed wine. They may still be waiting.

And the Balance of Nature eventually was restored.

EPILOGUE

Colin wasn't used to failure. He wasn't exactly used to success, but more to a sort of 'middle-of-the-road, avoid anything that might be a little risky or require too much thought' type of action.

This made the next few days even harder to bear than usual. He had effectively risked all to go to Threa, had not really seen any good friends too badly killed, for a change, and in fact had even created a couple of new ones. And he had been so close to bringing home his loved one that it hurt real bad. He could now understand all those pop songs about love hurting; there was an ache in his very soul which wouldn't go away. It hurt terribly, deeply and awfully.

He went through the motions of his life mechanically; getting up in the mornings, dodging the mugs and going to work. He would robotically stamp books, sort shelves and listen without notice to Brian's inane comments. And all the time he thought of Cozzie. His darling Cozzie. His true love, the only girl for him. Her face eventually misted from his mind to leave a startling image of soft, yielding flesh that had often stuck his sheets together by morning.

Colin would spend hours in front of the Crime and Catastrophe section knowing that for all the earth and people and animals and plants beyond it and over the horizon there was also Cozzie. She was a million light years away and yet somehow, tantalizingly, just around the corner.

Many a time Brian had to shoo Colin away from those beautifully dusted and sorted shelves with a loud whisper to go work on another section of the library, snort har. For Colin tended the Crime and Catastrophe section with a tenderness that anyone could have mistaken for love. If he couldn't have Cozzie then he would keep her gateway clear. Just in case.

Oh sure, she'd had a fling with that Niloc character, but it was really only a substitute for a romance with the missing Colin as far as Cozzie was concerned, he knew that.

At home he was listless, forever fidgeting and moving around without being aware of his surroundings, as if he had a deep-seated discontentment with his lot. At work he moped and stared. He had a pain through his heart that just wouldn't go. In fact, nobody noticed anything unusual about him until he strode purposefully into the library one Saturday morning, thirty minutes late.

'Tsk tsk, young Colin, we're ... what are we? H'mm?' hissed Brian, who was obviously peeved at having to do the first check-out shift himself.

'We're pissed off with all this shit!' yelled Colin at him, indicating the general area. This time the words came out exactly as he had intended, and no Throbulets cluttered up his pathway. He had a serious gleam in his eye and a maniacal grin on his lips. He wore a towel wrapped around his hips in the manner of a loin cloth and nothing else. Absolutely nothing.

For Colin had reached a decision that morning. He had decided that he no longer belonged to the planet Earth, if he ever had done so before. No, he belonged to Threa, and to Cozzie and he was going back there for good and he wouldn't even tell his parents he was going.

Brian and his two regular Saturday early customers, old Mrs Edwina Bush and old Mr Arthur Gash (no relation and certainly not Beaver warrior women of the Syorks tribe, though an incredible coincidence none the less. A portent, maybe. An omen.) looked on incredulously as Colin marched up to the Crime and Catastrophe section and strode straight into the shelving.

The onlookers were even more astounded to see the bookcases crash to the floor, taking the Wars, Battles and Bombs section with them. Colin bounced backwards and ended up sitting on the floor, legs akimbo, and with a stunned look on his face. His nose bled and he had lost his towel. One lense of his glasses was cracked.

As Colin threw himself repeatedly onto the flattened shelves and piles of books he became more and more upset, and his sobs turned to screams as he failed to find the portal. He got splinters in his hands and feet, twisted his ankle and sprained both wrists doing a swallow dive into the floor, but still remained firmly rooted on Earth.

All the while he was yelling, 'I want to go back, Oh God, I want to go back!' and he was still yelling this when PC Dave Clarke, the local bobby who had been following the more-or-less naked Colin through town on his bike, finally caught up with him and started to restrain him using the minimum of force necessary to subdue a herd of rampaging elephants.

Colin looked up through the bloody haze in his eyes and his swollen face cracked into a grin. Bits of teeth flew out as he spoke.

'Ken Clarke! Ken Clarke!'

'No sir,' explained the portly PC Clarke as he plunged his fist once more into the dumbly smiling Colin's face. 'Dave, not Ken, sir, and I would like you to accompany me to the station sir, if you don't mind.' He dragged Colin away in a head lock, past the immobile Cann, Bush and Gash at the check-out.

Nobody noticed the Throbulet snout poke out from the floor of the library just where the Crime and Catastrophe section used to be and sniff the air for a moment. Nor did anyone notice it grasp a copy of *How to make your own Tactical Nuclear Warhead* and disappear back into the floor with it.

Colin would be off work for three months, part of it in hospital getting over what was officially diagnosed as a breakdown, but which he knew was a broken heart.

It took Brian ages to clear up the mess in the library.